DANGEROUS *Games*

Also by J.T. Geissinger

Dangerous Beauty Series

Dangerous Beauty
Dangerous Desires

Slow Burn Series

Burn for You
Melt for You
Ache for You

Bad Habit Series

Sweet As Sin
Make Me Sin
Sin With Me
Hot As Sin

Wicked Games Series

Wicked Beautiful
Wicked Sexy
Wicked Intentions

DANGEROUS
Games

A DANGEROUS BEAUTY NOVEL

J.T. GEISSINGER

Published by Montlake Romance, Seattle

www.apub.com

Amazon, the Amazon logo, and Montlake Romance are trademarks of Amazon.com, Inc., or its affiliates.

ISBN-13: 9781542007726
ISBN-10: 1542007720

Cover design by Letitia Hasser

Cover photography by Reggie Deanching

Printed in the United States of America

To the man from National City who blackmailed me for a kiss.

Whoever fights monsters should see to it that in the process he does not become a monster . . . if you gaze long enough into an abyss, the abyss will gaze back into you.

—Friedrich Nietzsche

No one saves us but ourselves. No one can and no one may. We ourselves must walk the path.

—Buddha

A wise woman once said, "Fuck this shit," and lived happily ever after.

—Anonymous

ONE

Eva

"Make a sound and she dies."

His gun pressed to the woman's temple, Dimitri speaks in Russian, his voice as soft as silk. His smile says he assumes I'll obey his instruction, because experience has taught him that I will.

This is an old game between us, one I know well. A game called Do What I Say, or Someone Innocent Suffers.

In this case, the someone innocent is a terrified stranger holding a bottle of wine who Dimitri used as a lure. She really could be the woman who owns the Airbnb rental Naz and I checked into, which she identified herself as when I asked through the closed door of the apartment moments ago, but I'll probably never know.

Because her brains are about to paint the porch red.

Sorry, lady. I stopped taking orders from this asshole a while ago.

My scream is a wild beast of a thing, tearing out of my throat with fangs and claws. It's long, loud, and composed of a single word.

"Naz!"

The woman jumps, drops the bottle of wine, and bursts into hysterical tears.

Dimitri is so stunned by my disobedience that he simply stares at me in blank disbelief.

I take advantage of his surprise and kick him as hard as I can in his balls.

He doubles over with a roar but doesn't drop the gun. The woman shrieks like an air-raid siren. Naz calls out from somewhere behind me, a panicked shout, but my attention is caught by the sound of heavy boots pounding up the wooden stairs to the second-story apartment. I only have time to scream Naz's name again before a group of armed men dressed all in black swarm the landing at the top of the stairs and crowd there shoulder to shoulder.

Dimitri's soldiers point a forest of handguns at my face.

The woman's eyes roll back into her head, which makes a dull thud as it hits the landing's iron rail on her way down to the floor. She flops sideways, unconscious, legs splayed. Her plaid housedress rides up, exposing flabby thighs the color and texture of curdled milk.

"Take her!" snarls Dimitri through gritted teeth. His eyes blaze cyborg blue, but he's still doubled over, cradling his groin.

I spin around to run but am caught by my T-shirt and yanked backward. My back bumps into a solid surface. A forearm as hard as an iron bar snaps into place around my throat. I scream again, struggling and clawing at the arm that holds me, but my scream is cut short as the arm tightens like a vise.

As stars pop in my vision, Naz emerges from the bedroom with his gun in his hand.

He strides toward us, arm outstretched, fully nude and heartbreakingly gorgeous.

"Stop where you are!" shouts Dimitri in English.

Apparently he's recovered from my attack on his balls, because he jerks upright and shoves the barrel of his gun under my jaw. My teeth clack together with the force of it.

Naz freezes in place. His eyes are black and wild. His hair is wet. He's dripping with moisture from the shower, his body gleaming, his chest heaving up and down with each breath.

Each labored, fury-filled breath. I can almost taste his rage. It's a sharp metallic tang in the air, dangerous enough to cause spontaneous combustion.

There's a moment of electric silence where the only sound is the harsh breathing of the man who's holding me. His mouth is so close to my ear that his hot breath is a wash of steam down my neck. Then Naz takes a careful step forward, and Dimitri speaks.

"Yes, come closer. If you want her dead."

Naz freezes again. He's focused on Dimitri with extraordinary intensity, his eyes unblinking and his jaw like stone. He appears to have no self-consciousness about his nudity and no fear that he's staring down a dozen muzzles of loaded guns. Every muscle in his powerful body is tensed, ready to strike.

He's magnificent. David challenging Goliath, the light of vengeance in his eyes.

Please, God, don't let him be about to die!

My heart throbbing wildly, I cut my gaze to Dimitri. He gives Naz a cold, purposeful once-over, then says to me in Russian, "Stop fighting and come with me quietly, or I'll blow that horse cock of his clean off."

"If he dies, you won't have any leverage left!" My words sound strangled because of the pressure on my voice box. I cough, gasping. "My only purpose in life would be to kill you!"

"I have a suspicion that's already your only purpose, Evalina, but in any case, a man can survive having his cock shot off."

His faint smile tells me he's done that particular bit of nasty business himself, many times.

"Shoot him, Naz! Kill this bastard!"

Dimitri slices me a lethal look. "Not only disobedience, but also name-calling. I see I'll need to reteach you manners."

His voice vibrating with fury, Naz says, "If I shoot him, they shoot you."

"How astute, Mr. Mansouri." Switching to English, Dimitri turns his attention back to Naz. "You always were bright, if a little near-sighted. Now let me be clear so there are no misunderstandings. I'm taking Evalina. She belongs to me. If you follow when we leave, or make an attempt to take what's mine from me, or in any other way interfere with my property, she pays the price. I'll send her back to you one piece at a time, starting with her tongue."

His smile turns cruel. "As I'm sure you've discovered, it's the least useful of her body parts."

The air around Naz shimmers with his rage. When he looks at me, entire planets are burning in his eyes. His look says *I love you. Stay calm.*

I wonder if he sees my horror and helplessness, made a million times worse by the realization I had only moments before I opened the door that it's possible I'm carrying his child.

Dimitri gives a command for his men to retreat. Everyone starts to move slowly as one unit. The man holding me drags me back one step, then another. My bare feet kick helplessly as I fight him, desperate for air.

Dimitri snaps, "What did I say about fighting?"

When he points his gun at Naz, I fall still, a scream of terror trapped in my throat. "No! Please!"

Hearing me plead makes something ugly glitter in the depths of Dimitri's cold blue serpentine eyes.

This is what he wants from me, what he's always wanted. Begging. Weakness.

Fear.

He feeds on it the way a vampire feeds on blood.

I realize there's only one way out of this. There was only ever going to be one way—I see that clearly. All the months I've been running and hiding and falling in love were only ever going to take me right back to this moment, facing down the darkest of my demons.

We can try to bury the past, but some corpses refuse to lie quietly in their graves.

In a way, it's a relief. I don't have to worry any longer about the worst happening, because now it has. Now all I have to do is focus and pray for strength.

I speak in Russian because I don't want Naz to understand my words. "I promised you my soul in exchange for time with him. But if you pull the trigger, I won't have a soul left to give. If you kill him, you kill me, too, and all this will have been for nothing."

With a warning in his voice, Naz says, "Eva."

He might not understand the words, but he hears my bargaining tone. My heart feels as if it's dying.

Looking into Dimitri's eyes, I say hoarsely, "I haven't forgotten how to please you."

Dimitri's pupils dilate. He moistens his lips.

And oh, what a dangerous game I'm playing. What a dark, dangerous game. But I might have more than Naz's life or my own to think of protecting now, and the sooner Dimitri believes I've submitted to him fully and without reservation, the sooner I can find a way to drive a stake through this devil's heart and rid myself of him forever.

Dimitri fists a hand into my hair and kisses me, thrusting his tongue deep into my mouth.

I'm aware it's a test, a test I must pass or Naz will die, but it still takes every ounce of willpower inside me not to wrench my head away and spit, to remain passive and still as if bile isn't rising in my throat at the revolting taste of him.

When Naz makes an animal sound of fury, Dimitri breaks away from my mouth, laughing.

"Oh, the jealous lover. What fun! It'll be torture for you, won't it, imagining all the ways I'm going to fuck her? All the ways I'll make her scream and beg?"

Naz's nostrils flare. His chest expands, and his lips flatten. His fingers tighten around his gun.

Dimitri laughs again, delighted. "I'm sorry I won't be here to see you suffer, but I'm afraid we have to be going now. Eva and I have some catching up to do. Remember what I said: if you follow us, she pays the price."

Just to put an exclamation point on that threat, he smashes the butt of his weapon into the side of my face.

My head snaps sideways. I hear the crack of bone and feel something hot pour down my cheek, but I don't make any noise because agony has stolen my voice. When I sag, the man holding me from behind wraps his other arm around my waist to keep me from falling.

Naz's roar of helpless rage raises all the tiny hairs on my body.

Then I can't hear anything else because the thunder of gunfire deafens me.

The man holding me jerks and staggers backward, releasing me abruptly from his grip. The acrid stench of gunpowder burns my nose. Brilliant flashes of light blind me. I fall to my hands and knees, gasping and disoriented. Blood rains onto the white carpet beneath me, but I don't know if it's mine or someone else's. I can't focus my right eye, and the light is starting to dim.

The shooting goes on forever. Reality takes on a dreamlike quality. Everything turns muted and fuzzy, as if I'm seeing it through a pair of dirty glasses. Someone grabs me by the scruff of my neck and drags me across the threshold onto the landing, then gives me a hard shove in my back.

I teeter at the top of the stairs for a moment, weightless, breathless. Then gravity takes over, and I tumble forward and down, my arms pinwheeling, my mouth open in a silent scream.

I hit the first step. With a sickening snap, a bone in my left arm breaks. The world spins topsy-turvy. I continue to roll, hitting what feels like every stair on the way down to the ground, where I land on my back.

My skull cracks against the unholy hardness of cement. The wind is knocked out of me, and for a moment my vision goes black.

When it clears, I'm looking up at the night sky, dotted with stars. My head lolls sideways. Through the iron bars of the fence that encloses the yard on the ground floor, I meet the glassy gaze of the big angry dog Naz and I thought would alert us to any danger.

He lies dead in a pool of his own blood, a perfect circle blown through the middle of his furry forehead.

A powerful wave of emotion overwhelms me. Sorrow for this poor creature that got caught up in Dimitri's web and disgust at myself for being the fly Dimitri would chase to the ends of the earth. If it weren't for me, the dog would still be alive, happily terrorizing passersby with his ferocious barking.

If it weren't for me, Naz would be safe.

If it weren't for me, a lot of things would be better.

Then I hear my mother's voice in my head, chastising me as she used to do when I was a child.

Self-pity is a luxury people like us can't afford, Evalina. Don't ever feel sorry for yourself. It's the most useless of emotions and the most addictive of drugs. Spend too much time wallowing in your sorrows and you'll drown.

"I won't drown," I promise the dead dog, my voice the weakest whisper. "And I swear Dimitri will pay for what he did to you."

I'm going to make him pay for everything he's done, to everyone.

The distant wail of sirens fills the night. I'm aware of people nearby, talking to one another in shocked voices, a small crowd of neighbors gathering to find out what all the noise is but not daring to get close. I look up the stairs just in time to see Dimitri stumbling down them, holding his side, his face contorted in pain. Bodies of men are piled on the landing, but two of Dimitri's soldiers are still standing. One of them slings Dimitri's arm over his shoulders and supports him as they descend. The other, a few steps ahead, makes a beeline for me.

He picks me up and throws me over his shoulder.

I groan and almost pass out from the pain, but manage to stay conscious.

"Hurry!" shouts Dimitri.

The soldier carries me across the street to a parked van. Upside down, I catch a glimpse of the stairs, expecting Naz to emerge from the open doorway of the apartment, but there's no movement up there. He's not in the window, either, peering out at us, and the sound of his voice doesn't echo through the night.

A bolt of anguish slices through me like a sword.

No! Naz! NO!

I hear the sound of a heavy door being thrown open on metal rollers, then the soldier tosses me into the back of a cold, dark van. He slams the door shut behind me. It closes with the hollow finality of a lid sliding onto a coffin.

I look around frantically. There are no windows. Thick wire mesh extends from floor to ceiling, caging me into a few cramped feet of space.

I find the strength to shout Naz's name into the darkness, but my shout is met only with the sound of more doors opening and closing at the front of the vehicle. When the van's engine roars to life, I holler his name at the top of my lungs, hoarse and desperate, my heart banging against my rib cage, terror burning like wildfire through my veins.

With a squeal of tires, the van lurches forward. Dimitri's voice comes to me from the front of the van, but it might as well come from my worst nightmare.

"You can forget about him, Evalina. He won't be coming after you anymore. He's dead."

We speed off into the night with Dimitri's dark laughter the soundtrack to my screams.

TWO

Eva

We drive. For a hundred years, or so it seems in my frigid cocoon of darkness. All the while, I hyperventilate, curled into a ball, my eyes wide open and staring at nothing as my mind runs on a hamster wheel of horror and denial.

Naz can't be dead. Dimitri's lying.

But Naz would never let you go if he were alive.

He must be injured. Yes, that's it—he was injured and couldn't make it to the door in time to follow us. He'll come for me soon. He'll always come for me. He promised he'd always keep me safe.

You fool. Dead men can't keep promises.

Eventually, the van jerks to a stop. Doors open and close. Men's voices murmur somewhere outside, then the back door slides open.

The soldier who threw me into my cage now takes me out, handling me with more care than before when he sees the ugly angle at which my arm is bent. I cradle it against my chest and allow him to help me climb out and get my footing.

We're at a small airfield in the middle of a plain that stretches as far as the eye can see into blackness, a blackness that matches the color of my soul. A gleaming jet awaits a few dozen yards away with its engines running and airstairs extended down to the tarmac.

The soldier says, "Go on. He's waiting."

He visibly winces when I look up into his face. I must look like death. The thought gives me a morbid sort of satisfaction.

I don't bother trying to run. There's nowhere to go. I'm headed to my fate, a destination no one can escape, and everything good I may have had is far behind me.

Maybe not everything, whispers an urgent voice inside my head. *There's no proof Naz is gone, but even if he is, you might have his child inside you. Don't give up yet.*

I close my eyes, swallowing around the rock in my throat. Anguish wells up inside me, making it almost impossible to breathe. Of all the terrible things life can throw at us, surely the worst of them is hope.

"Gospozha?" says the soldier.

The English equivalent is "madam." It's a sort of honorary, a polite form of address for a woman, and the thing I was always called by Dimitri's underlings in my former life as his favorite.

I guess some things never change.

But some things do.

I'm no longer the girl I was before. The girl who ran away from a monster and fell in love with a god. I have blood on my hands and a wasteland in my heart and the memory of Naz's beautiful smile branded on my mind, a memory Dimitri Ivanov is going to regret I ever formed.

Because it's the fuel that will drive me forward until the moment I burn his whole world to the ground.

I open my eyes, stand up straighter, and take a deep, steadying breath. "I'm ready."

An odd expression crosses the soldier's face.

It's probably my imagination, but it looks like fear.

The interior of the jet is the definition of the word *ostentatious*. Everything is black leather, black lacquer, or gold leaf, except for the plush carpeting, thick pile the color of oxblood. On one wall is painted the Ivanov family crest, a gold arched crown encrusted with jewels and topped by a cross on a checkerboard background of blue and yellow.

Looking at it, I spit on the oxblood carpet.

"Another new bad habit?" says Dimitri. "I've got my work cut out for me."

He sits stiffly in a chair down the aisle, just outside the closed cockpit door. He's pale and sweating. Beneath his open suit jacket, his black dress shirt is saturated with blood.

"If you don't die of that gunshot wound first."

He smiles coolly. "You know very well it would take far more than a bullet to kill me."

Despite his injury, he's in control of himself. He hasn't even loosened his tie.

I should be terrified or furious or experiencing something else other than this strange detachment I feel. I suppose it must be shock. Either that or all my brain capacity is tied up dealing with the agony of my broken arm and smashed face, which has swollen so badly I can't see out of my right eye.

"Sit down," he commands, "and let me look at you."

I hesitate for only a moment, out of a useless flare of rebellion, but then take the seat across from him and gingerly settle back into the comfort of buttery-soft leather. Then I lift my eyes and meet his gaze and simply sit and stare at him.

Those red lips, as plump and pouty as a girl's. That glossy blond hair. That classically handsome face, fine-boned and aristocratic, with its innocent aspect and pleasing symmetry of features.

It's said that Lucifer was the most beautiful of all the angels, before he betrayed God and was cast out of heaven. Sitting across from me is undeniable proof that the most lovely of things can hide the greatest of evils.

After a long time, Dimitri says, "First, truth. You knew I'd find you. Yes or no."

I breathe in. I breathe out. I manage the urge to shriek and gnash my teeth like one of those undead creatures in a horror movie, ravenous for brains.

"Yes."

Oh God, that sickening smile. That smug, sickening smile.

"Do you know why you were always my favorite, Evalina? Why I would chase you across thousands of miles and go to so much trouble to get you back, when it would've been so much easier to simply dispose of you?"

I consider it. The monster is in a generous mood, the man I love could be dead, and all the world is ashes. Might as well play this dark game to its end. "Because you can't stand to lose?"

"No."

When he doesn't continue, I say, "Is this multiple choice, or are you going to tell me?"

"Because of all the women I've ever had, only you have proven to be unbreakable."

Unbreakable.

There's an echo of an unmet goal in his tone, the excitement of a game hunter talking about the man-eating tiger he dreams of tracking down and turning into a stuffed trophy for his wall. When I swallow, a fine tremor running through my hands, his smile turns sinister.

"'The green reed which bends in the wind is stronger than the mighty oak which breaks in a storm.' Confucius said that."

"How illuminating."

He ignores my bitter sarcasm. "You're my green reed, Evalina. I saw it the first time I laid eyes on you. You danced out onstage at the

Mariinsky Theatre all those years ago, and my heart stopped, because I knew I'd found what I'd been looking for."

I grimace, my stomach curling into knots. "A slave?"

"No," he breathes, his eyes glittering. "An equal."

The laugh I produce is sharp and ugly. "Putting aside for a moment how ridiculous that is, you kept me like a dog. In a cage. With a collar. You did unspeakable things to me, things I can still feel right now sitting here talking to you. Don't try to make it sound like anything more than it is: *you got off on my pain.*"

"Trial by fire," he says, sounding reasonable. "There's no other way to determine if the clay you're molding will crack unless you put it into the kiln."

I stare at him in disgust that's only outweighed by disbelief. "So I'm the pottery and you're the potter?"

"I admit it's a rough comparison."

"You're completely insane. You realize that, right?"

"Am I? Look at yourself. You're sitting there composed, even defiant, though at least one of your bones is obviously broken, your eye is swollen shut, and your lover was killed in front of you. Without the experience of your years with me, you'd probably be curled up in a corner, catatonic with pain and grief."

"Your lover was killed in front of you."

Breathe, Eva. He's the prince of lies. Just breathe.

Through gritted teeth, I say, "I suppose you think I should thank you for that."

He lets his gaze drift lazily over me. "You can show me your gratitude later."

"Oh, I'll be showing you something later for sure, but it won't be gratitude."

He cocks his head, examining my expression with a clinical look of interest. "You really loved him, didn't you?"

Loved, past tense. If he's lying, he's being very careful.

I have to look away for a moment to compose myself. I'd rather die right here than let him see me cry. When I can finally speak, my voice is tight with hatred. "I told you what would happen if you lost your leverage."

"Yes. Your only purpose in life would be to kill me. Terrifying."

He sounds bored. Then, after a moment, he asks, "Why are you smiling?"

I turn my head and meet his gaze again. "You underestimating me is going to be fun."

I expect fury. What I get looks closer to arousal.

Then he leans forward and snatches my broken arm in an iron grip, and the scream of anguish that rips from me is like a banshee's.

He drags me from the seat to the floor and leans down close. "We're going to have *all kinds* of fun, my love," he says in a throaty whisper as I writhe at his feet, crying out in pain. "Just you wait and see."

"Oh. Pardon me, sir."

A man stands to our left in the aisle. He's balding, wearing glasses and a nice blue suit with polished oxford shoes. He's carrying a large black bag in one hand. He looks like an accountant.

Dimitri releases my arm and relaxes into his chair, but not before giving me a brutal kick that sends me sprawling into the aisle. I roll to my back, gasping in agony, trying not to vomit.

The man with the black bag looks dispassionately down at me.

Dimitri says, "Leave her. Take a look at this."

He stands, shrugs out of his jacket, loosens his tie, pulls it over his head, and unbuttons his shirt. He tosses everything on the chair I just occupied and allows the man with the black bag to inspect the hole in the side of his abdomen.

I swallow and swallow, choking back moans, cradling my arm and fighting to stay conscious. The pain is so intense it's the only thing I can concentrate on, a white-hot burning point of misery that blots out everything else.

Then ancient habit kicks in. I retreat to that place inside my head where nothing can reach me. The place I found one night in a hospital bed during my first horrific year with Dimitri, the dark little hideaway where I know I can survive.

From far away, I hear Dimitri's pleased laughter.

"That's right, little reed. Go ahead and bend."

He gives me another brutal kick, just for good measure.

⚬⚬⚬

A Rachmaninoff piano concerto plays over the jet's speakers as the doctor attends to Dimitri's bullet wound, and I lie curled and lifeless on the floor like a dead leaf dropped from a bough in winter.

Only I'm not lifeless. Not really. Inside the prison of my broken body, my heart still beats.

Naz. Naz. Naz.

Every heavy thump wails his name. Every bone and sinew screams out for him. Every breath I take bears witness to the impossibility of my existence in a world where he's not by my side.

Or is he? Is he still out there living and breathing and desperate to find me? Is my grief one more move in Dimitri's dark chess game?

The unknowing is torture. I squeeze my eyes shut tighter and swallow the whimper rising in the back of my throat.

"Set that bone in her arm and see to her face," Dimitri says to the doctor, who must be finished attending to his wound. "But no painkillers. She hasn't earned them yet."

The doctor murmurs his assent. He sounds neither surprised nor repulsed, simply deferential. He's a man comfortable in the presence of other people's pain.

I feel a light touch on my shoulder. When I don't respond, the doctor says, "If you sit up, it will be easier for both of us."

His tone is conversational. He's prepared to set my broken bone with or without my assistance. I'm considering if I want to comply or kick him in the nuts when that awful hope rears its head again, reminding me that it would be wiser to save the fighting for when it matters most.

I open my eyes. Swallowing a moan, I push myself upright.

With my back against one of the seats and my knees drawn up, I look at the doctor. He's crouched in front of me, examining my forearm. It's black and blue, grotesquely swollen, and bent at a hideous angle. Dimitri stands down the aisle a ways, buttoning up a fresh dress shirt over his bandaged waist.

One corner of his mouth is curved up.

I recognize that telling curve. It's anticipation. He can't wait to hear how loudly I'm going to scream.

You soulless bastard. You will never, ever get a single scream out of me again.

If hearts are capable of turning to stone, mine just did.

I look the doctor in the eye. "Let's do the arm first."

He makes a dismissive sound and shakes his head. "I should clean and stitch that cut under your eye first. If I start with the arm, you might pass out before I can take care of your face."

Looking at Dimitri, I say, "Do. The. Arm."

The little upward curve of his mouth fades and is replaced with a dissatisfied quirk.

Finished buttoning his shirt, he tucks it into his trousers, then dons and adjusts his tie, cinching it tight around his neck. Then he sits down, crosses his legs, smooths his tie down his chest, rests his hands lightly on the armrests of the chair, and gazes at me.

I hold his gaze as the doctor runs his fingers down the length of my arm, quickly and efficiently probing the injury, then presses his thumb and forefinger against my wrist and counts my pulse. I hold his gaze as pain shoots through me in nauseating, stabbing waves. I hold his gaze as the doctor says, "Closed proximal fracture of both the ulna and radius. You're lucky the bones didn't break the skin. Wiggle your fingers for me."

I move all my fingers, still holding Dimitri's gaze.

His eyes reveal nothing. His expression and posture are both serene. Only a single finger betrays him. His right index finger begins to tap a slow, steady beat against the arm of the chair.

The doctor says, "It appears your nerves are unaffected. If you need surgery, you can't have it until the swelling goes down, but in the meantime, I'm going to realign the bones. This will hurt. Tell me when you're ready."

I won't scream. I won't allow myself to scream. I. Will. Not. Scream.

"I'm rea—"

The doctor snaps my broken bones back into place before I can finish the sentence.

Withering heat flashes over me. All the blood drains from my face. I suck in a hard breath, my eyes widening. The pain is so intense I think I'll topple over.

Instead, I lean into the aisle and vomit all over the plush oxblood carpet.

I retch and spit while the doctor patiently holds my arm, on his knees in his nice blue suit. When my stomach is emptied, I sit upright again, panting. I'm shaking. A cold bead of sweat snakes down my forehead and drips into my eye.

The doctor seems unsurprised by my reaction. "I see you had vegetables for lunch."

I say hoarsely, "Vegetable soup."

Dimitri's still staring at me, but his finger has stopped tapping, and the upward curve of his mouth has returned.

The mechanical airstairs fold up, and the cabin door closes. The jet's engines grow louder. The doctor applies a splint to my arm and fashions a sling for it, then removes a small bottle of antiseptic and a piece of cotton gauze from his bag and begins to dab at my cheek.

Then a beautiful raven-haired stewardess in a short skirt and sky-high heels appears from behind a black velvet curtain at the back of the plane.

She looks at me. She looks at the doctor. She looks at Dimitri, then at the chunky yellow pool of vomit on the floor. Then, with the glassy stare and blank expression of a person so used to horror she's no longer able to be moved by it, she says, "We'll be taking off momentarily. I'll clean up the mess. Would anyone care for a drink?"

Dimitri says, "Let's open the magnum of Cristal. I feel like celebrating. My lost little lamb has found her way home again."

His smile comes on slow and full of malice.

The plane lifts off. The doctor stitches the cut on my cheek, then promptly falls asleep in a seat by a window. The stewardess mops up my vomit from the carpet, serves Dimitri champagne, then sinks to her knees on the floor in front of him and unzips his trousers.

Over the rim of a Baccarat crystal flute, Dimitri watches me with heavy-lidded eyes as she takes his erection into her mouth. He fists a hand in her hair and forces her down on him until she's gagging.

And back into the monster's twisted kingdom I go.

THREE

Eva

It's raining hard when the jet touches down, the inky sky emptying itself in fat freezing drops that soak me as I walk barefoot and shivering to the Phantom waiting across the tarmac from the jet.

Dimitri walks beside me, the back of my neck grasped firmly in his hand.

A uniformed driver hurries toward us with an umbrella. Dimitri waves him aside and instructs him to open the door. When he does, Dimitri shoves me in first, then follows, sitting beside me and smoothing back his hair as I huddle in the corner. The driver closes the door and jumps back into the car, and we pull away.

After a few minutes, I glance over at Dimitri. He's staring out the window at the rain-slicked passing night.

"Where are we going?"

"You'll see."

His expression is neutral, but his tone is rough, the way it gets when he's excited.

He has good reason to be. He's caught his escaped pet rabbit and is bringing it back to its pen, where he'll conduct experiments to see exactly how much pain the little bunny can take before it dies.

But if the bunny's smart, it will keep him calm until it can get its hands on a weapon.

I glance away and moisten my lips, my heart a trapped humming-bird beating against the cage of my chest. "How did you find me?"

His laugh is soft and short. "So full of questions. You've forgotten how much I dislike questions."

He turns to look at me. A passing streetlight illuminates an unmistakable bulge in his lap, and I turn away, sickened. I resist the urge to shrink against the door.

Obviously his appetite wasn't slaked by the stewardess.

"I dislike these clothes, too."

He reaches out and touches my T-shirt, then trails his finger down the bare skin of my arm. When I freeze, my skin crawling, he makes a small sound of satisfaction deep in his throat.

His voice silky soft, he says, "Do you know how much I want to fuck you right now, Evalina? How much I want to rip off those rags and curl my hands around your throat and fuck you while I listen to your strangled screams? Hmm?"

My mouth is too dry to answer. I sit in tense silence, listening to the drum of rain on the roof.

He chuckles. "Yes, you do." He makes another sound, closer to a moan than a sigh. "You've always known what I want. I've missed that." His voice drops an octave, turning husky. "I've missed that sweet cunt of yours, too. So sweet and tight. Or did your dead lover stretch it out with his big cock?"

I form a crystal clear mental image of Naz making love to me, cradling my face in his hands and whispering his devotion as he spilled himself inside my body and laid claim to my heart and soul.

A tidal wave of grief and fury crests inside me, burning hot, obliterating all rational thought and curdling my blood to poison. "Yes, he stretched me out. If you fucked me now with that tiny dick of yours, it would be like sticking a baby carrot up an elephant's ass."

I see the driver's eyes widen in the rearview mirror. He glances back at me and our gazes meet, but he quickly looks away, as if he's afraid to be caught looking at me or suffer my same fate.

But Dimitri surprises both of us by laughing.

"What a charming visual. You always did have a sharp sense of humor. Did he make you come?"

His tone is light, but he's flipping over stones, hunting for weaknesses. Soft spots where he can press down with his thumbs. I bite my tongue and look out the window, but my silence only serves to intrigue him.

He leans over and grasps my jaw, forcing me to look at him. "Answer me."

He'll know if I'm lying. He always does. So I tell him the simple truth, my voice raw with emotion. "Yes."

He lets his gaze drift over my features, soaking in my pain. Wallowing in it like a pig in shit. Then his rosebud lips curve into a cruel smile. "Tell me about it."

He slides the heel of his other hand along the bulge in his crotch.

My pulse goes haywire. I'm caught, trapped between competing impulses of fight or flight, knowing instinctively that I'm being presented with a way to hold off treatment even more horrific than what's about to happen.

He was right: I do always know what he wants. And what he wants now is for me to tell him a story. A very particular, explicit kind of story. If I do, I'll be granted a reprieve from further beatings.

Or worse.

I moisten my lips and steel my nerves. "I . . . liked it. It felt good."

He blinks slowly, his eyes growing hot. "What did he do that felt so good?"

"He liked to put his mouth on me. He liked to use his tongue."

Dimitri's fingers tighten around my jaw. His hand moves restlessly between his legs. "Go on."

"He would . . . kiss me there—"

"Where?"

"Between my legs."

The rip of a zipper opening. Dimitri's hand fumbles into his trousers, finds what it seeks, makes a fist. "You let him eat your pussy?"

"Yes."

His hand strokes up and down, fondling his jutting erection. He breathes, "Slut. My pretty little slut. You loved it, didn't you, his greedy mouth on your cunt?"

I choke back a sob and whisper, "Yes."

Dimitri's hand slides down my jaw to my throat and squeezes. He's so excited his hand is shaking. The other one is busy between his legs.

He prompts, "And then?"

"Then . . . he would fuck me."

Dimitri exhales a soft little moan, his hand moving faster.

"Sometimes hard. Sometimes soft. But always deep."

"He had a big cock," he whispers, so close to my face his hot breath stirs my hair. "Did he make you suck it?"

Hot and acidic, bile rises in the back of my throat. I'm on the verge of tears, but I can't give him the satisfaction. "He didn't make me. I wanted to."

"You *wanted* to." Astonished.

"Yes. I wanted to please him."

He groans, flexing his hips in time to the strokes of his hand.

I squeeze my eyes shut and speak rapidly, knowing Dimitri is nearing his climax, knowing what he needs to get there, and knowing the sooner he does, the sooner I'll be released from this hell.

"I would get on my knees and take him into my mouth and suck him until he was close, and then he would put me on my hands and knees and fuck me from behind, or I'd get on top so he could fuck me and squeeze my breasts—"

A long, low moan. Dimitri arching in his seat, straining.

"He loved my breasts," I say, tearing up, my voice breaking. "He always wanted to kiss them. He liked to bite my nipples, just hard enough to sting."

Dimitri sucks in a breath.

I whisper, "But sometimes hard enough that he'd leave teeth marks on my skin."

With a groan and a shudder, Dimitri orgasms, tightening his hand so hard around my throat I gag.

He jerks a few times, grunting, then sags against me, panting onto my neck. His hand around my throat slackens. I cough, desperate to catch my breath.

Then his mouth is on my neck, hot and wet, making me cringe in disgust.

"Good girl," he says, breathing heavily. "My gorgeous good girl. You never disappoint. My God, I've missed you."

Don't cry, Eva. Stay strong. Don't you dare cry.

I keep repeating it silently to myself as Dimitri slumps back into his seat with a satisfied sigh. He flips open a compartment in the armrest of the door on his side and withdraws a hand towel, which he uses to clean himself up. Then he reaches in again, this time producing a small white plastic bottle. He shakes out two oblong blue pills into his hand and wordlessly offers them to me.

Painkillers.

Now I've earned them, but what harm might they do to the speck of life I might be carrying in my belly?

Worse, what harm might Dimitri do if he suspects the speck of life exists?

I take the pills and set them under my tongue, pretending to swallow.

After a moment, Dimitri says, "What do you think you're doing?"

Shit. If he gets suspicious, it will end in disaster, so I flip the pills over and swallow, this time for real. "It's hard to get them down without water."

We drive in silence as he inspects my profile, and I sit stiffly in my seat, praying to God for deliverance.

He doesn't seem to be listening.

⤬⤬⤬

When we pull to a stop a while later, I'm inhabiting a black and desolate place inside my head. It takes several tries with increasing volume for Dimitri to get through to me. His voice sounds as if it's coming to me from underwater.

"Evalina. Evalina, wake up."

He snaps his fingers in front of my face, but I wasn't sleeping. Just gone for a stroll through the tangled darkness of my mind.

Naz, please be alive. Please.

"I'm awake," I hear myself say, as if from far away.

My sense of detachment is a gift, one that keeps on giving as Dimitri exits the car and rounds the rear to open my door. Extending his hand, he smiles at me. A demon's smile, sharp and menacing, promising me a front-row seat in hell. His perfect blond hair gleams like a pearl in the moonlight.

I clasp his fingers and allow him to help me out, but when I try to stand, I stumble and fall to one knee. Gravel digs sharp teeth into my kneecap.

"My little lamb is feeling weak," he says, enjoying the idea. He nudges me with the toe of his shoe. "Can you walk, or do I need to drag you inside by your hair?"

I force myself to my feet, fighting back a wave of nausea. Despite the pills, my arm is throbbing, my cheek is hot and tight around the stitches, and I ache in the places he kicked me.

Far worse is the ache in my chest from the ragged hole where my heart used to be. It hurts like a phantom limb, missing but not forgotten, taking relentless jabs at the blanket of dullness my mind has wrapped itself in. It takes all my willpower to stand silent and upright under his gaze.

"You suffer so beautifully," he notes, his eyes glittering. "Such stoicism. But you won't be able to keep it up for long. I've been anticipating our reunion for months." His smile grows venomous. "Plenty of time to get creative with your punishments."

He curls hard fingers around my good arm and yanks me forward. I yelp in pain, stumbling. The icy gravel cuts into the soles of my bare feet.

Then I look up and catch a glimpse of the cage that awaits me.

Dracula's castle couldn't be any more frightening.

Peaked towers stab black daggers into the sky, obliterating starlight. A thousand dark windows consider us with hostile, glinting stares. Stately and sprawling, spookily lit by moonlight, the mansion looks like one of those places with ghosts in the attic and carnivorous monsters lurking in a labyrinth hidden deep beneath the floors.

Like a cornered cat, my soul recoils, hissing and bristling at the sight.

"What is this place?"

"Your new home."

We don't ascend the cracked marble stairs leading through the withered gardens to the main entrance, but instead take a detour around the north wing, walking under an arched colonnade festooned with gnarled dead vines until we arrive at a large wooden door. It's plain and windowless, set back into vaulted stone, and flanked on either side by burly bodyguards gripping machine guns.

They snap to attention when they see us.

"Open it," orders Dimitri as we approach.

One of the men produces a large round key ring from inside his suit jacket. He picks out one of the many skeleton keys on the ring, fits it into the lock, then flattens a beefy hand on the door and pushes. He steps aside to let us pass, his face a slab of stone.

The door swings shut behind us with a muffled boom and a cold draft, making the candles gutter in their brass candelabras lining the bare limestone walls. Cobwebs flutter in the shadowed ceiling corners.

"Oh, this isn't creepy at all," I say, standing beside Dimitri in the dank gloom. "Are you taking me to the Pit of Despair?"

"Shut up."

His tone is icy. He doesn't get my *Princess Bride* reference. The only man who would might be lost to me forever.

I swallow, thankful for my mental detachment, because it's all that's keeping me from sliding in howling agony to the floor.

Dimitri tugs on my arm. We descend a twist of uneven stone stairs, the temperature dropping with every step. I smell moss and rot and mouse droppings, hear the faraway trickle of water. The steps are so cold beneath my feet it burns.

Hysteria threatens the edges of my unnatural calm, but I push it back, offering a silent prayer to Jude the Apostle, patron saint of lost causes. But he and God must be on the same extended vacation, because when we reach the bottom of the spiral staircase, there's no salvation to be found.

What greets me instead is my own personal hell.

"Do you like it?" inquires Dimitri, his tone as gentle and stroking as a caress. "When the estate was first built, this was used as a wine cellar, but it's been empty for decades. I had it specially prepared just for your return."

The room is small, round, and furnished like a prison cell, with nothing more than a narrow bed covered in a rough gray blanket, a metal stand holding a porcelain bowl filled with water for a sink, and a black cast-iron pot on the floor that I assume is a toilet. Windowless stone walls stretch up into deepening gloom. There are no lighting fixtures, mirrors, or running water, and nowhere to sit except on the bed or the bare floor. The only light comes from a beeswax pillar set into a niche over the bed. Judging by its height and the way the flame is weakly wavering, it doesn't have long left to shine.

I close my eyes, inhale a breath, and put everything I was behind me. Until I know for sure what happened to Naz, and if the speck of life in my belly even exists, the one thing—the *only* thing—I have to do is survive.

I open my eyes and look at Dimitri. "Are you planning on leaving me to rot here until I die?"

His answering smile would make the devil himself quake in fear.

He turns and makes his way back up the twisting stone stairs. The heavy wood door opens and closes. The key turns in the lock.

I sit on the bed and stare at the walls until the candle gutters and burns out, and I'm left alone in darkness as cold, black, and silent as outer space. Then the grief and hysteria I've been holding back crashes over me, and I throw back my head and scream Naz's name.

From outside the locked door comes the sound of faint, satisfied laughter.

FOUR

Naz

It's a funny thing, being shot. It can really ruin an otherwise wonderful day.

I lift my head and look down at myself, then wish I hadn't. I'm covered in blood. I can't tell where the holes are, or how many there are, but the pain is a demonic entity that's taken over my entire body. Searing agony pulses in waves from my toenails all the way to the top of my head. I feel like I was chewed up and shit out by a velociraptor. Every breath is pure torture.

But the pain doesn't matter. The only thing in the world that matters is Eva. I need to clear my head and move fast.

I'll worry about how Dimitri found us later. If that bastard Killian had anything to do with this—

Stop! Focus! Get your ass in gear!

Pushing both the pain and the panic aside and forcing myself to concentrate, I sit up and take inventory.

My right calf has a ragged gash where a bullet nicked the flesh. It's leaking blood like a sieve, but it's not a serious wound. More problematic is the hole in the left lower quadrant of my abdomen. It's leaking badly, too, but as I gingerly probe the area with my fingers, I discover an exit wound in the back, which is good.

I mean, "good," all things considered. From the feel of it, the bullet missed my rib cage, and all the major organs of the region are higher up. I can tape up the hole and be functional.

At least until my colon leaks bacteria into my abdominal cavity and sepsis sets in.

The biggest problem is the wound in my chest.

It's on the right side, beneath my clavicle. So at least my heart isn't involved. But the degree of difficulty I'm having drawing a full breath suggests one of my lungs is probably fucked.

I hear the distant wails of sirens drawing nearer at the same time I realize I've got a pile of dead guys littering the landing and the foyer.

Then half a dozen Germans in black trench coats burst in, brandishing weapons.

"Good timing, assholes!" I rasp, infuriated. "Where were you five minutes ago?"

They ignore me, jumping over the bodies of Dimitri's men and spreading out through the room in formation, sweeping the area for the danger they completely missed.

I've gotta talk to Connor about his European assets. They're not exactly the sharpest tools in the shed.

One of the Germans—the tallest one, with a platinum crew cut and silver rings on both his thumbs—crouches down next to me. Gazing at my naked, bloody body, he shakes his head. In English, he says, "I've seen swiss cheese with fewer holes."

His accent is heavy, and so is his sarcasm. I'd like to pop his eyeballs out with my index fingers, but the sirens are getting closer, and the panic I'm trying to fight back is having a field day with my nervous system.

"Help me up."

He shoves his weapon into a pocket of his coat and hoists me up with his hands under my armpits, intelligently not making any comment at my groans of pain or my inability to support my own weight once I'm upright. I lean heavily against him, sucking air through my teeth.

He shouts something in German to his companions, who all come to stand in front of me and stare at me like I'm livestock in a farm auction.

I bare my teeth like an animal. "Yeah, soak it in, assholes. This mess you're looking at is your fault. If you'd had my six like you were supposed to, I wouldn't have so many fucking holes!"

One of them shrugs. "I'm hypoglycemic. We stopped to eat."

I send him a baleful glare. "If I don't die, I'm gonna kill you."

He has the balls to look offended. Then he says prissily, "Well, that would be very inconvenient for you, as I'm the one who got the license plate of the white cargo van with blacked-out windows that just went speeding down the street." He purses his lips. "I wonder who could be in it."

My shock is so total I nearly drop dead. "Call it in to Metrix so they can track it, you fucking moron! What the hell are you waiting for?"

Outside, the sirens crescendo. What sounds like an entire squadron of cars screech to rubber-burning stops. I see through the balcony windows that the walls of the apartment building across the street are lit up with flashing red-and-white lights.

Cops.

Fuck.

The only way out is down the front stairs, right toward them.

When I let out a bellow of frustration, the tall German supporting me rolls his eyes. "You Americans are so dramatic. I'll take care of this."

He hands me off to one of the others and strides out the door, stepping nimbly over corpses, then disappears down the stairs.

"He's going out to greet them?"

When I stare after him with my jaw unhinged, the prissy one says, "Don't worry about it. Günter has friends in high places."

I don't have time to ask how high, because my brain decides it's had too much of the punishing pain and blood loss bullshit and now would be a great time to take a leave of absence.

The room narrows to black, and I fall.

⤟⤠⤡

I awaken sometime later with a jolt, my heart hammering as if it's been kick-started with a defibrillator.

I'm in the back of an ambulance with a white sheet draped across my lower body. We're tearing down the street at top speed, swerving, sirens blaring.

Sitting calmly on a narrow cot across from me is Killian, impeccable in the same expensive suit he wore for our meeting at Saint Stephen's Cathedral earlier in the day.

"Question," he says, seeing that I'm awake. "Why are you naked?"

I bellow, "Where's Eva? What's happening? If you had anything to do with Dimitri finding us, I'll kill you!"

Amused, he gazes at me with his eyebrows lifted. "You have a lot of energy for someone who should be dead."

When I lunge at him, rolling halfway off my cot in the process, Killian shoves me back with a hand flat on my chest and curses.

"Calm down! You'll hurt yourself more than you already are!"

I'd like to tell him to go fuck himself, but I'm too busy groaning in pain. I lie flat on my back with my eyes closed, making noises like an animal that got hit by a car and is dying on the side of a road.

"Aye, that's more like it. Now if you can shut up for half a second, I'll talk."

Through a clenched jaw, I say, "Eva. Start there."

31

His sigh is big and dramatic. He removes a silk pocket square from his suit jacket and wipes my blood off his hand. "Jesus, Mary, and Joseph. I've never met two more stubborn people in my life."

The ambulance careens around a corner, tires squealing. The driver seems to be in an incredible hurry. I must be worse off than I think.

Killian says, "I intercepted a call from your German friends to Metrix headquarters relaying the situation—"

"You spied on the Germans? How?"

"I'm a spy, that's how. Be quiet. As I was saying—"

"Dimitri took Eva. You need to let me out of this ambulance. I'm gonna get her back."

"Excellent plan," he says drily, tossing the bloodied square of silk aside. "You seem in perfect shape to be giving chase to an armed madman surrounded by armed bodyguards."

"I've been worse." I force myself to breathe through my nose so I don't pant like a dog. It's incredibly hard to maintain a normal breathing pattern when your body thinks it's dying.

"I see. And will you be putting on a pair of trousers before your attack, or were you planning on wrestling Dimitri in the ancient Greek style? Which he might actually like, by the way."

"Fuck you, Killian."

He exhales, shaking his head in disapproval. "I have no idea what she sees in you. You're extremely short on charm."

"You said earlier you had a high opinion of me."

"I only said that to get on her good side."

When I glare at him, he sighs again. "I'm joking. You make it too easy for me, mate."

"My sense of humor takes a nosedive where you're concerned. And I'm not going to any hospital, so stop this fucking ambulance and let me out."

"I never said we were going to a hospital."

We stare at each other as the ambulance takes another sharp turn around another corner, knocking me against the wall and nearly dislodging Killian from his seat.

"Really? Then are we in a car chase I don't know about? Because this driver's a maniac."

"I told him I'd give him a thousand euros if he got there in under ten minutes."

"There? Where's *there*?"

The sirens cut off, the ambulance comes to a screeching stop, and Killian smiles. "Here."

When the driver throws open the back doors, I see we're in a warehouse of some sort. A big metal door is rolling down silently behind us. The ceilings are high, the lights are low, and there's a strange electrical humming emanating from some large piece of out-of-sight machinery.

The place has a vibe like a serial killer's lair.

Killian says sourly, "Don't look at me like that. I didn't take you here to murder you. I would've just let you bleed out back where we came from if I wanted you dead. This is one of many safe houses I keep.

"And to answer your earlier question, no, I had nothing to do with Dimitri's arrival. I should be offended that after all we've been through, you still don't trust me, but I know what a suspicious arse you are."

He jumps out of the ambulance, then he and the driver—a swarthy dude with a goatee who's so hairy he looks like he's wearing a pelt under his white T-shirt—pull me out on the cot.

"A chop shop?" I look around in disbelief at dozens of expensive cars in various states of dismemberment. "What are you gonna do, trade my organs for engine parts?"

"We're gonna get you field ready, bro," says Swarthy Goatee. "I'm Doc, by the way."

"Doc? Oh, fantastic. That makes me feel one hundred percent better. I'm sure you got your medical degree from Harvard, right?"

He and Killian share a glance. Killian says, "Ignore him. He's always premenstrual."

I want to shout something about how sexist that is, but the room begins to spin and red starts to pulse in my vision, so I close my eyes and concentrate on my breathing again.

"I'll start a saline drip," says Doc in a conversational tone, "then clean you up and get some X-rays so I can see what we've got."

I give him a quick rundown of the injuries I already noted and the caliber of bullets I think were in Dimitri's men's guns. Then I open my eyes and look at Killian, walking beside my cot. "He took her. He walked right fucking in and *took* her."

I have to stop talking because my throat has closed.

Killian knows the real meaning behind my words, how guilty I feel. Instead of blame, he offers support.

"She's tough. She survived seven years with him. She'll survive awhile longer. And don't bother beating yourself up over it, because I counted nine dead men in that apartment. You did your job, mate. Not even I could've done better. By all logic, you should be dead, too."

Thank God I had the high-capacity magazine in my Glock. It's possible I'm hyperventilating, but at this point I don't care. "I need to talk to Connor. One of the Germans said he got the license plate of a van—"

"I know. And your friend Connor already traced the plates. They were stolen from an Audi that belonged to a suburban mother of four."

"Fuck. Did they check the traffic cams? Could they follow the van after it left our location? Do we know where they went?"

"Yes to all three."

Doc parks the cot in a makeshift operating theater, with monitors, bright hanging lights, and various machines bristling with cords and tubes, then goes about setting up the saline drip. I can't concentrate on anything else other than the sound of my heartbeat thundering in my ears.

I shout, "And?"

Killian regards me warily, a muscle jumping in his jaw. "Take a deep breath."

"Oh shit."

"Aye. They lost the van just outside the border of the Czech Republic. They went into a tunnel, and there were no traffic cameras on the other side. Satellite turned up nothing."

Panic flares like a firework inside my chest. She's gone.

Eva's gone.

This time maybe for good.

"However . . ."

Killian's pause gives me a huge surge of hope. I jerk up onto my elbows and holler, *"However what, asshole?"*

Doc chuckles, shaking his head.

Killian pulls one of his business cards from an inside pocket of his suit jacket. He holds it up between two fingers.

Exasperated by his unnecessary air of mystery, I demand, "What? Did she call you? What're you saying?"

"I'm saying that there's more than black ink embedded in this high-quality cardstock."

I stare at him, feeling like I'm about to pass out again, only this time from relief. "GPS?"

He nods. "Micro-thin, state of the art. Outside the café we went to after the cathedral, Eva put my card into the back pocket of her jeans, remember?"

What I remember is that I nearly tore the thing in two and threw it in his face because I was furious with him at that time. He'd been poking me with a stick the entire afternoon. Now I'm so grateful I could hug him.

"She was wearing those jeans when Dimitri took her."

"And I've got a blinking green dot on one of my monitors that confirms it." He nods to a hacker's setup on the other side of the warehouse, a U-shaped desk surrounded by glowing computer screens and racks of blinking CPUs.

"Oh God. Oh fuck. We haven't lost her." Limp with relief, I flop back onto the cot and drag in a few ragged breaths.

"Aye. Bask in that for a minute."

The tone of his voice alarms me. "What's that supposed to mean?"

"It means they're in the air."

That's bad, but not too bad, considering Tabby will be able to track the plane now that we have a bead on it. But when Killian just stands there looking at me, I know there's more. "This cloak-and-dagger routine isn't doing me any favors. Just tell me."

He slides the business card back into his suit pocket and folds his arms over his chest. "To conserve battery life, the card is off-line until it's taken beyond a certain geo-fence zone. As you know, GPS is a huge battery hog, and as you can guess, a device sized for concealment in a business card is miniscule. Once the system goes live, the clock starts ticking."

All the relief I felt a few moments before evaporates. "How long do we have before the battery in Eva's device runs out?"

He glances at his watch. "Just under three hours."

I look at Swarthy Goatee. "You got any drugs on hand that'll gimme enough juice to stay on my feet for that long?"

He looks at me like I'm nuts. "I haven't even x-rayed you yet!"

I sit up, gritting my teeth against the wave of pain that wants to take me down. "Skip it, Doc. Just staple up my holes and gimme the meds. We're working against the clock."

When he throws his hands in the air and turns to Killian for help, Killian simply gazes at me.

"Fine with me. If you die, I'll happily step in and take care of Eva for you."

I stare at him for a moment, at his square jaw and perfect nose, then lie back down. "Okay, Doc. Do your thing."

I'll wait until he's finished to tell him I'm gonna need his clothes.

FIVE
Eva

Alone in the dark, a minute is a year.

I don't know how long I sit on the cot, lost in my thoughts, after the sound of Dimitri's laughter fades, but eventually the cold gets to me, and I start to shiver uncontrollably, teeth chattering. Instead of curling up under the rough gray blanket, I walk slowly across the room, hands outstretched, until I reach a wall. I follow the curve around, moving blindly in the dark, cursing when I stub my toe on a stone step.

Then I make my way, inch by inch, up the uneven spiral staircase to the landing at the top.

The tall candles are still burning in their candelabras. I blow out all of them except one, then gather them up and carry them back down to my cell, ignoring the drips of hot wax burning my arm.

I stack the unlit candles on the floor near the cast-iron pot, set the lighted one into the guts of its burned-out kin in the niche over the bed, and take a long look around at my cage. It's as dreary and inhospitable as a medieval dungeon.

Well, it could be worse. I haven't seen any rats yet.

I want to take off my jeans and try to rest for a while, but the thought of Dimitri arriving while I'm asleep and half-clothed stops me. It's then, thinking of my jeans, that I remember.

I've got Killian's business card in my back pocket.

I whip it out and stare at it, breathless with some unnamed emotion that has my heart racing and my hands trembling.

"You'll never be allowed near a phone," I say, my voice echoing off the walls. "Even if he lets you out of here, Dimitri won't let you out of his sight long enough for you to make a phone call."

Unless . . .

I squeeze my eyes shut. *Unless I earn his trust.*

The thought makes my stomach churn. But I won't think of it now, what hideous acts earning his trust will involve. Instead, I commit the number to memory, mouthing it silently over and over until I'm sure I can recite it in my sleep.

Then I hold the edge of the card over the candle flame until it catches on fire.

When the flame has eaten half of the card, I set it on the stone floor and watch until there's nothing left but a smoldering curl of black ashes. I scoop up the ashes and dust my hands off over the cast-iron pot, blowing away any remaining smudges from the floor.

The acrid smell of burned paper hangs in the air, along with an odd metallic aroma I can't identify. Something that smells like melted wires.

With nothing left to do but stare at the walls, I stretch out on the cot, pull the blanket over me, and close my stinging eyes.

⌘

I wake to total darkness.

"Shit." I bolt upright, my pulse erratic. The candle burned out an hour or a year ago, and I won't be able to light another. Dimitri left no matches behind.

What about his men?

I'm sure the bodyguards outside—if they're even still stationed there—will be under strict instructions not to open the door. But perhaps I could coax one of them to pass a lighter through one of the chinks in the stone threshold?

It's a safe bet to assume one or both of them smoke, as many men stationed for long periods of time in one position do, to keep alert and combat boredom. Though the two guarding my door are unfamiliar to me, most of Dimitri's men smoke. Almost as much as they drink.

Decided, I creep carefully across the room, as blind as an earthworm. I know the general heading of the stairs now, though, and find the first step soon enough. I hurry upward, shivering but grateful for the cold because it seems to be helping the swelling in my cheek area. The stitches aren't quite as tight, and the skin around them no longer feels hot.

My arm I don't dare touch. God only knows what's happening under the splint. I wouldn't be surprised if I never regain full use of it again.

When I reach the landing of the stairs, I press my ear to the door and listen with held breath for any sign of life.

". . . beautiful girl, though. *Amazing* tits. And those lips. Woof."

"Are you fucking stupid? I told you already, shut the fuck up about her."

"What else is there to do out here but talk? Who's gonna hear us, the crows?"

"How do you know we're not on camera? You think he'd leave a piece of ass like that out here alone with us without keeping an eye on what we're up to? Use your head."

"Psh. You worry too much."

"Yeah, and that's why I'm still alive."

The men speak with a dialect common to those from the southern part of Russia, a hardening of the final consonants that's distinct.

"I gotta take a piss," says the one who's discontent with all the chatter.

Which is lucky, because that leaves the one who likes my boobs behind. If I'll have a chance with anyone, it's him.

I count to ten to make sure the other one has left, then knock on the door. "Hello? Anybody out there?"

The shuffle of feet. A cleared throat. I imagine him looking furtively around.

"I was wondering if you had a match or a lighter I could borrow. My candles have burned out."

The silence stretches so long I don't think he'll answer, but then my heart leaps when I hear his voice, low and close to the door.

"I can't talk to you."

"I understand. I won't tell anyone. We don't have to speak again. It's just . . ." I make my voice wavering and thin. "It's so dark in here. I don't like the dark."

A heavy exhalation, or maybe it's the wind. After an eternity, he says, "Don't make me sorry I did this."

I look down. He's pushing a red plastic disposable lighter under the door.

I kneel down and snatch it before he can change his mind. "Thank you!" I whisper. "I'm so grateful to you!"

A noise like a satisfied grunt.

"What's your name?"

After a moment's hesitation, he says, "Vlad."

Like Vlad the Impaler. How apropos. "Oh, that was my father's name! It's my favorite!" Both lies. I hope my voice doesn't sound as brittle to him as it does to me.

When he doesn't respond, I think our conversation is over. But then he says, "What's your name?"

I drop my voice an octave, trying to sound winsomely vulnerable and scared. "I'm Evalina."

He repeats it, a husky note in his voice. He's thinking of my boobs.

I say breathily, "Thank you again, Vlad. You're an angel. I won't forget you helped me. When I get out of here, if there's anything I can do for you, I will."

That grunt again, as if he's already compiling a list.

"What're you doing down there?"

His companion's sharp voice carries from however far off he is, returning from relieving himself. I stand abruptly and hold my breath until Vlad says, "Thought I heard a noise. But it was nothing."

He lies much better than I do. His voice is casual and untroubled, as I imagine his expression to be as well. The other man says, "It doesn't matter if she screams her fucking head off—it's none of our business, you hear?"

"Yup," says Vlad easily. The subject is closed as his friend starts bitching about the cold.

I slink back down the staircase with my prize clutched like a cross in my hands, my head buzzing with all the ways I might use Vlad's appreciation to my advantage, never guessing such an innocent every-day item as a disposable lighter could bring such disaster crashing down onto my head.

∞

It begins, as many nightmares do, with a crack of thunder.

I jolt upright, startled out of a deep sleep by the sound of an approaching storm. I'd been dreaming of Naz, of chasing after him on a deserted beach, crying out his name in vain as he ran faster and faster ahead of me, until he disappeared into darkness without ever looking back.

It takes a moment for me to reorient myself, even less than that for me to realize I'm not alone.

Dimitri and the two bodyguards stand at the bottom of the staircase, staring at me.

His voice so mild it's almost disinterested, Dimitri says, "Ah. Sleeping Beauty awakens."

A viper coils around his words, flashing sharp fangs.

I pull the blanket close to my chest, my blood quickening in my veins. The guards are tense, too, their faces wary, their fingers white-knuckled around the stocks of their machine guns. My mouth turns as dry as bones bleached in desert sand.

Whatever this is, it's bad.

Stepping forward, Dimitri smiles. He's wearing a beautifully cut suit of black silk—always, always black silk—and the ubiquitous black tie. He looks refreshed and in utter control, all that nasty gunshot business put firmly out of mind.

I've never known another person with such a high tolerance for pain.

Except, I realize with skin-crawling distaste, myself.

"So how are you faring down here in your cozy little space, my love?" Dimitri lifts a corner of the blanket, fingering it idly as he speaks. "Comfortable? Finding everything you need?"

As if on cue, my stomach grumbles. I keep my face blank and my gaze on Dimitri's polished shoes. "I need food."

"Ah, yes," he answers thoughtfully. "Since all the other basics are covered. Shelter. Water."

His pause feels dramatic. I glance up at him, the hair on the back of my neck standing on end.

He lets his gaze wander around until it lands on the candle flickering in the niche over my bed. His smile widens. "Fire."

Vlad shifts his weight from foot to foot. I want to scream at him for his stupidity.

Dimitri sits on the end of my bed, crosses his legs, and drapes one wrist over the other as if he's on a social call in a fine parlor waiting for a maid to hand him a cup of tea. Every line of his body is relaxed.

Only his eyes give him away, that burning cold glow of glacial blue.

He says, "Evalina, is there anything you'd like to tell me?"

Solicitous. Like a concerned parent.

It's obvious he knows about the lighter, but this little game delights him. Thrust, parry, feint, stab and stab at your opponent until they bleed to death from a thousand cuts while you spin away, laughing.

All right. If it's games he wants, it's games he'll get.

After all, I learned from the master.

"Why, yes, there is," I say in that same solicitous tone. "In all seven years we were together, you never once made me orgasm. But I suppose the victim's pleasure isn't the goal of rape."

Dimitri's expression remains unchanged, but the bomb explodes on the bodyguards' faces. Their shock is so total the room echoes with it.

But I know Dimitri too well. He's got his eye on the brass ring, and not even a direct insult to his manhood in front of underlings will budge it.

"Your manners are atrocious," he says, flicking an invisible piece of lint from his sleeve. "I'll deal with that later. But you know very well what I was referring to."

"I do. I didn't want to bring it up in front of company, dear, but if you insist."

He glances at me, waiting.

"Your halitosis has gotten completely out of control. It's crop-wilting at this point. Every time you speak, I'm not sure if you need a breath mint or toilet paper."

"Funny," he says, deadly soft. "But I'm talking about the lighter."

So there *are* cameras. Hidden somewhere in the dark so Dimitri could spy on me. I should have guessed.

Vlad falls still.

Don't react! Let me handle this!

I try to send it to him telepathically, but he doesn't receive the message. His face pales to white, and his throat works. He swallows reflexively, taking a slow step back.

"You didn't leave me matches," I say, holding Dimitri's gaze. "You knew I would ask. You set this up. You can't blame anyone but yourself."

"Oh, but I can. And I will." Dimitri stands, shooting a lethal glance at Vlad.

Weary is all I feel. Tired to the marrow of my bones. I'm sick to death of carrying so much fear, of enduring so much violence, of everything to do with this childish, sadistic bully.

If you're testing me, God, I'm sick of that, too.

I stand, let the blanket fall, and face Dimitri fully. "I'll take his punishment for him."

The slight upward curl of Dimitri's lip tells me he already knew I'd do that. Vlad and his friend stare at me as if they can't decide if I'm a miracle or insane.

Dimitri clasps his hands behind his back and begins to pace thoughtfully at the end of my bed, as if in deliberation, as if he hasn't already seen this entire sordid thing to its end. I want to shout at him to cut the crap, but so far his temper is holding, and any sudden loud noises might push poor Vlad over the edge. I don't feel like being riddled with bullet holes.

So I stand there and wait while the viper furls and unfurls his shiny black coils, delighting in the ways he makes his puppets dance.

"All right," he says finally, stopping to pull himself upright. He gazes down his nose at Vlad with an air of disappointment. "What you've done is a breach of my trust, but I assume you're willing to make amends."

Vlad nearly prostrates himself in his relief. "Yes, sir, please, yes, anything."

Anything. The moment the word leaves his lips, I know it's a mistake.

I'm proven right when Dimitri turns to me, lit up like the sun. He reaches behind himself, under his suit jacket at his waist, and produces a thin black length of metal, folded in thirds. With a practiced flick of his wrist, he snaps the whip open, locking it into place.

He holds the whip out to Vlad, who takes it, looking confused.

Dimitri and I stare at each other. Neither of us is confused about what's going to happen, but only one of us is smiling.

Poison dripping from his fangs, the viper says to me, "Strip."

SIX

NAZ

"You must have a guardian angel looking out for you, man, because none of these wounds are life-threatening. The bullets didn't hit any major organs, blood vessels, or bones."

"If I have a guardian angel, that fucker drinks."

I'm flat on my back on the cot, feeling like a bag of smashed assholes, desperate to get up and get going because the X-rays, ultrasound, and other parts of Doc's exam have already taken way too much time.

Every second I'm apart from Eva is a lifetime.

"What's the deal with my lungs? It hurts to breathe."

"The blast wave from the bullet is traumatic to soft tissues and hollow organs, but you caught another bit of luck in that you were hit with small-caliber, full-metal-jacket ammo. If they'd had rifles with hollow points and you were hit in the same spots, you'd be a goner. Your organs would've been liquefied."

"So my gut's not as bad as it looks?"

"It's a clean in-and-out, man. No perforation of the small bowel. No bullet shards in the wound. Internal bleeding is minimal. I'm telling you, it's a miracle."

Somehow I don't feel blessed.

"I'm gonna start you on antibiotics for now to make sure infection doesn't set in. You'll need to be stationary until you're fully stabilized and no secondary issues show up."

"Secondary issues?"

"Gunshot wounds are sneaky. What looks straightforward can turn real fast into something catastrophic."

"How long will it take before we know if I'm outta the woods?"

"A few days, at a minimum."

"That's way too fucking long!"

Doc shrugs, turning away from the black-and-white picture of my abdomen he's been peering at on a laptop hooked up to the X-ray machine. "Or I let you go now and you could die in a few hours from anything from hemorrhage and infection to shock. Up to you."

Sitting on a stool nearby and looking like an ad for the latest James Bond movie, Killian says, "You're no good to her dead, mate."

"Fuck!" *Eva. Sweetheart. Hold on.*

"Dude, it's a miracle you're even breathing. You should be stoked."

I squint at Doc, confused by the contradiction of his looks—which are Middle Eastern—his accent—which is some murky mix of Southern California surfer and vaguely European aristocrat—and his attitude, which is nerdy professor. He's amorphous, like fog.

"Where are you from?"

Without a hint of irony, he answers, "Earth."

"Great. Now I've got two abstruse assholes to deal with."

"Abstruse?" Doc lifts his brows. "I don't even know what language that is."

"When he's not shouting obscenities at people, he likes to read a thesaurus," says Killian. "He could've said 'hard to comprehend,' but then he wouldn't feel smarter than you."

Exhaling hard, I drop my head onto the cot and close my eyes.

Killian says, "Stop plotting my death. We've got plans to make."

"I wasn't plotting your death. Just a little light dismemberment that would leave you alive but without any limbs."

"So basically a stump?"

"I'd float you in a pond and call you Lily."

"That's disturbing, mate."

"You know what's really disturbing? You calling me 'mate' every five seconds. Cut it out."

"I hate to interrupt this adorable bromance you've got going on," says Doc, "but I need to stitch you up."

"Like with a *needle*?"

"Like with a needle."

"You don't have any QuikClot around the Batcave?"

"No."

"Fuck. Fine, we'll do it old school."

"I'll give you a shot of local anesthetic before I start."

"No, just hurry up and get it over with."

"Dude, it's gonna hurt."

"I don't want any drugs!"

He rolls his eyes. "Of course you don't. Congratulations, you're macho. Hold still and keep quiet."

He starts with the wound in my upper chest, working slowly and methodically, then moves to the exit wound in my shoulder, then moves to my belly.

It takes a long time. Forever, it feels like. With every tick of the clock, a winch winds tighter in my gut, until I'm drawing short, ragged breaths, my whole body shaking.

He has her. He took her. I failed.

I hear Killian's low voice just as I'm about to leap up from the cot.

"He'll be preoccupied getting somewhere safe. We've got a wee bit of breathing room."

Before Dimitri does anything really vile to Eva, he means. Which of course we don't know.

I answer in a raw voice, my eyes closed. "You didn't see the pictures. What he's done to her in the past. The abuse . . ." I have to stop and take a few deep breaths, desperate to scour the images of Eva's injuries from her hospital file that are flooding my head, but they just keep on coming. "He'll be itching to make up for lost time."

"He's got too many other important things on his plate. My guess is he'll put her on ice for a while."

There's a certain knowing tone in his voice that makes me open my eyes and look at him. "The nuke?"

He nods. "Dimitri has to ensure the dust settles on that pile of dead soldiers of his you left behind at the apartment before he makes any moves to complete the transfer of the warhead. When the police discover the men worked for him, he'll get a lot of heat."

If Doc is surprised by the turn in the conversation, he doesn't show it. He just keeps on stabbing my flank with a needle, cheerfully sewing, as if working on a nice piece of fabric and not a bag of meat.

"None of them will have ID. They can't be traced back to him."

Killian scoffs. "No, they won't be carrying their passports, but likely most if not all of them will have arrest records from one country or another. Once their corpses are fingerprinted, it won't take much digging to find their known associates."

His smile is faint and annoyingly self-confident. "And if the authorities need a little nudging in the right direction, I'll be happy to help."

He delivers that last line as if he's all-seeing, all-knowing Mr. Super Spy at your service, thank you very much. His arrogance really chaps my ass.

"About that. I've been meaning to ask you."

He cocks his head.

"Who the fuck *are* you?"

He waves a hand in the air as if swatting away a fly. "You already asked me that."

"Yeah, I did, and you slung me some humblebrag bullshit about how you were 'no one of importance.'"

"Bullshit? So you think I'm important? I'm flattered."

"I swear to God, I've never met anyone more irritating than you."

"Need I remind you, Nasir, that I recently saved your life? You could show a bit more gratitude."

My laugh is incredulous. "You're taking credit for saving my life?"

Doc snorts. "Right? *I'm* the miracle worker here, not him."

I ignore him, too busy glaring at Killian. "The Germans showed up before you! They would've taken me to a hospital!"

Killian says mildly, "But they didn't take you to a hospital, did they? I did." He waves the hand again, indicating our surroundings. "Or something like it."

"I would've been just fine without you!"

"You would've been booked for murder without me. You need me, mate, whether you like it or not."

I holler, "What did I tell you about calling me that?"

Doc interjects again, pausing his jabbing to stare at us in exasperation. "Do you two lovebirds need a minute alone to canoodle, or can I please get on with my job?"

I'm derailed from the urge to break Killian's nose by the sudden jarring memory of Dimitri instructing me not to follow him or Eva would pay the price.

"What's that look?" asks Killian, sounding alarmed. "Are you dying?"

My mind turning, I say slowly, "No . . . but I should."

He looks at the ceiling. "And you accuse me of being abstruse."

"Before Dimitri left with Eva, he threatened that if I followed them, he'd send her back to me in pieces."

Into my thoughtful pause, Killian says, "I'm sure you have a point. Feel free to make it this century."

"If he thinks I'm dead . . ."

Catching my drift, he stands up straighter. "He won't be expecting you to follow him."

"Bingo."

Killian thinks for a moment, then nods. "It's genius."

Doc mutters, "You two girlfriends are giving me whiplash."

Ignoring him is becoming much easier. "Also . . . you should probably get arrested so he thinks you're out of the picture, too."

"Arrested?" repeats Killian, horrified.

"Unless you wanna be dead, too."

He sniffs like he smells something bad. "Aye, that's preferable. I can die with my honor intact, but arrested . . ." He shudders. "That's for amateurs. I have a reputation to keep."

"God forbid your gargantuan ego gets bruised."

He laughs at my tone, which burns with sarcasm. "Gargantuan ego? Excuse me, but people who live in glass houses, et cetera."

"Seriously, you two biddies are giving me a headache." Doc jabs at me with unnecessary ruthlessness.

"Ow!"

"Besides," continues Killian, sounding reasonable, "Dimitri doesn't know who I am."

"How does he not know who you are?"

"Did you think I called him up and gave him my real name and home address while I was negotiating to trade your girlfriend for a nuclear weapon? What kind of spy do you think I am?"

"Is that a rhetorical question? Because if not, I've got a *shitload* of answers."

"All smart-ass, no doubt."

"But accurate. Moving on, one of the Germans apparently has contacts high up, because he went out to greet the police before you showed up. I'll see if I can get him to get the cops to leak a story about an American dying in that gunfight. Dimitri might think I'm dead already, considering I was flat on the floor covered in blood when he

51

left, but a mention in the paper will seal the deal. It's not much, but it might make him lower his guard a little."

Killian nods. "In the meantime, I'll see if I can get any intel on how Dimitri located you. Someone somewhere is compromised, and I want to know who it is."

"It's not on my end, I can tell you that for damn sure."

He looks at me for a moment, his gaze inscrutable. "You never know, mate. Some people are very skilled at playing two sides against each other without either side ever knowing what's going on."

I narrow my eyes, suspicious, but he turns away, pulling a cell phone from his pocket. He paces to the other side of the warehouse and makes a call. He keeps his voice low so I can't hear what he's saying, which of course only makes me even more suspicious.

Then my gaze lands on the bank of computers.

I call out, "Hey, Killian?"

He glances at me.

"What does it mean that the blinking green GPS light on the computer just turned red?"

Killian strides to his desk and the bank of computer screens. He toggles the mouse, clicks a few buttons, then mutters an oath.

"What's happening?" I say loudly, panicking.

He straightens and looks at me. "Don't panic."

"Too late!"

"The GPS went off-line."

"Off-line?" I struggle to sit up, balancing my weight on my elbows. "How the fuck did it go off-line?"

"I don't know."

"Will it come back online?"

"I don't know."

I shout, *What* do *you know?*" then groan as a bolt of pain rips through me. I collapse to my back, panting, feeling electrocuted.

In a mocking falsetto, Doc says, "Oh no, I don't need anything for the pain. I'm a big macho idiot."

"Shut up!"

After a few moments where I try to breathe and Killian clicks around on his computer, he says, "For one thing, I know the exact coordinates of where the card was when it went off-line. And it had been stationary, which could mean it was their final destination."

"Oh sweet Jesus," I say hoarsely, relief coursing through me like rain. "I'm having a heart attack."

"Really?" says Doc, concerned. He lifts my wrist and starts to take my pulse, but I yank my arm away.

"Figuratively! Fuck!"

"Calm down, psychopath. All this hollering is bad for your blood pressure. You'll spring a leak."

I make a growling noise through clenched teeth that makes him roll his eyes again.

"We shouldn't get ahead of ourselves," says Killian. "Eva could've thrown the card out, changed clothing, submerged it in water . . . the possibilities are endless for why it was stationary and went off-line. There's no way to know without . . ."

He pauses. Looking at me all busted up and pathetic on the cot, he makes an apologetic face.

"Without going there," I finish for him, my heart sinking.

We both know I'm in no shape to be going anywhere at the moment, which means Killian is going after Eva alone.

Which, aside from her being with Dimitri, is basically my worst nightmare.

SEVEN

EVA

The frigid air of the cellar crackles with electricity as the two bodyguards stare at me in silence, waiting for me to follow Dimitri's command and remove my clothes.

If I don't, my clothing will be removed forcibly. I know Dimitri would enjoy it if I put up a fight. I'm not sure if he'd have Vlad strip me so he could watch, or if he'd do it himself, but either way, he'd savor every moment of my resistance.

Almost as much as he's savoring every moment of my hesitation.

I can tell from Vlad's horrified expression that he now realizes he'll be the one administering my punishment. He blinks rapidly, the whip gripped in his hand. His friend, however, seems intrigued by the drama unfolding. His brows are lifted, his eyes alight. He wasn't expecting such sport, but he seems to be looking forward to it.

Dimitri, for his part, is merely observing. Caesar at the Colosseum, watching with interest as the lions are led in.

"Give me your gun," says Dimitri to Vlad. "You'll need both hands free."

Vlad hands him the rifle. All the blood has drained from his face. I feel a strange sort of pity for him, ridiculous as it is. "It's all right," I tell him. "It's not your fault. Let's just get this over with."

Vlad swallows again. Dimitri exhales an impatient little sigh. From somewhere outside comes another distant boom of thunder.

I'm about to instruct Vlad to keep the blows away from my kidney area when he shocks everyone by speaking Dimitri's least favorite word.

"No."

For a moment, I'm sure I misheard. But then I catch a glimpse of Dimitri's face, his lips thinned to white and his nostrils flaring, and I know I'm not mistaken.

"I can't hit a woman," Vlad goes on nervously. "I'm sorry, sir, but I've never—"

The deafening crack of gunfire silences him.

I scream and dive onto the bed, covering my head. The sound of the machine gun firing in the small stone room is agonizing, like ice picks stabbing into both ears at once. Then the noise cuts off, and all that's left is the burned stench of gunpowder and an awful wet gurgling noise that I recognize instinctively even before I turn to look.

"You *are* sorry," says Dimitri, gazing down at the crumpled form of Vlad on the floor.

A ragged wound in his neck spits blood in a pulsing arc against the rough stone wall. His eyes are wild, his mouth gaping. His hands claw helplessly at his throat.

Sickened, I close my eyes and look away.

"What about you, Stefan? Where does your conscience sit on the subject of hitting a woman?"

The answer is unhesitating. "Your command is my conscience."

"Excellent. Evalina?"

When I look at Dimitri, he makes a gesture with his hand, indicating where he wants me to stand to receive my beating.

You have to survive. Think of the speck. Stefan will want to make a good impression he won't go easy he could really hurt you and you have to survive for the speck the speck the speck.

My mind is a blizzard of panic. My stomach is up in my throat.

Vlad might have been an ally, but Stefan definitely isn't. There could be far more here at stake than my pride. I need to do something drastic.

I slide off the bed and go to my knees on the floor in front of Dimitri. Head bowed, I say, "Master. Please forgive me."

If I thought the air was charged before, now it turns to fire.

Dimitri says, "Leave us."

He hands the weapon to Stefan, then Stefan's footsteps echo off the walls, growing fainter as he quickly ascends the steps. The big wooden door opens and closes, then I'm alone with the devil, kneeling at his feet.

He walks forward until the toes of his polished black shoes are an inch from my knees.

Vlad lets out a final soft gurgle. His hands flop lifelessly to the floor.

Then, for a long time, there's silence, broken only by an intermittent boom of thunder rolling across the sky.

"Look at me."

When I hear the heat in Dimitri's voice, a shiver of dread runs through my body. I glance up, heart pounding.

"It's a pretty picture you make, down there on your knees so appealingly submissive. But I've never required you to call me master. Why are you doing it now?"

I rack my brain for a clever answer but can't find one. "As long as you're alive, I won't be free. What else can that make you but my master?"

He's pleased by that, but disturbed by it, too. By the undercurrent of revenge running through the words like a poisoned thread. *"As long as you're alive.*" It's a threat gift wrapped in truth, and he knows it. But for some reason, it doesn't provoke his temper.

"You were never a slave, Evalina. You're still not."

I'm confused by that, and by his wolfish expression, the sharp expectancy in his gaze, as if he's been waiting for this moment. I thought a show of submission would buy me time, perhaps lighten my punishment, but he seems to have forgotten about my beating. There's something else, something darker, on his mind.

"What, then? A hostage?"

"More like . . . an apprentice."

For a moment, I'm blank.

Then a key inside my head fits itself into an old, rusted lock and turns. A door to an empty room creaks open, hinges groaning. I stand at the threshold, peering into darkness, looking for the monster that's always been waiting to emerge.

Frozen, I repeat, "Apprentice?"

Dropping his voice, he says, "You never wondered why I kept you so close? Why I allowed you to be present during business meetings? Why I tested you over and over to see what it would take to make you break? Think, Eva. You know I'm not a man who does things without good reason."

It isn't a monster that awaits me inside the room, but a painting. A picture on an easel, finger painted in blood by a murderer who laughed in delight at his own Frankenstein creation as it came to life under his hands.

Dimitri watches me closely, waiting for me to see the full picture. Waiting for me to discover the image of myself in the center, holding his hand.

And I do see. I see it with a clarity that burns inside my mind like a sun.

He's the potter. I'm the clay. All the years I thought I was simply being tortured, something far more sinister was taking place.

I was being *groomed.*

The air smells of blood. The floor is hard and cold under my knees. And inside the darkest place in my soul, an evil seed breaks into flower.

He tells people I'm his wife.

"Every king needs a queen," I say, gazing into the fathomless depths of his eyes.

His cheeks flush with excitement. "Precisely."

So here at last we come to it. The true price I'll pay for the foolishness of falling in love.

In the old days, before Naz, I would've wept. I would've cowered and accepted it as my lot. I would've been my mother's daughter and made the best of whatever disgusting thing life decided to throw my way, like slop to hogs. But now I see far beyond myself, into the future, a future where millions of people still live because I was presented with an opportunity to beat the devil at his own game.

A future where my child might live, too.

A future created by my willingness to do the unthinkable thing that must be done.

But I can't seem too eager, or this bloodhound will sniff me out.

"You know I hate you. You know you can't trust me."

"I'm not interested in your feelings, and trust is a commodity I don't deal in." He sends a wry glance toward the body of Vlad.

"Then what exactly are you proposing?"

He takes my chin in his hand, sweeping his thumb over my lower lip. "You've lived one quarter of your life with me. You grew from a girl to a woman under my watch. And look at you now. You're strong. Resilient. Unyielding, though it costs you so much. You're a warrior now, Evalina, because I made you that way. All that you are or ever could be is because of me."

I want to scream, but I wait, tensed, because I know more is coming.

"You've had a taste of freedom. I'll give you more, if you earn it. I'll give you almost anything you want, if you earn it." His voice grows husky. "Because you, and only you, know exactly what I need."

Yes, I'm intimately familiar with his needs. As I think of what he means by "earn it," saliva pools on the back of my tongue. I swallow so I don't spit. "I don't understand."

"It's very simple. You're going to marry me."

I jerk, so shocked I nearly fall over.

He's undisturbed by my reaction. "Or spend the rest of your life locked in this cellar."

He drops his hand from my face, turning away toward the stairs. He says over his shoulder, "I'll give you some time to think it over."

"I don't need any time."

He stops, pivots slowly, and stares at me.

Holding his gaze, I rise, until we stand facing each other with Vlad's cooling body the only witness to the Faustian bargain I'm about to make.

My heart in ashes, I tell the devil, "I'll marry you."

My answer is a show of gleaming white teeth.

⌘

As an engagement present, I get the whipping Vlad died for.

Breathing heavily, his forehead shining with sweat, Dimitri stands over the bed and my trembling, naked body. I'm facedown, panting in pain, my cheeks hot but dry. The rough gray blanket is twisted in my fist. My broken arm is agony. Welts burn blazing strips of fire up and down my legs, bottom, and upper back.

I didn't have to warn him to be careful of my kidneys. Dimitri knows how this is done.

He made me recite every transgression I've made since he found me at the apartment, starting with when I called him a bastard. It was a long list. He helped me along when I had any gaps in memory. Then he made me take off my clothes while he watched, his eyes like living fire. Finally, he made me thank him for the punishment I was about to receive.

The whole thing had an air of religious ceremony. The only things missing were a communion wafer and a gulp of sacramental wine.

I gave him everything he wanted without a hint of hesitation or reproach. Evalina 2.0, the girl who suffers any humiliation so she can lull the devil into lowering his guard.

I think I'll poison the bitch.

Picturing that, I make a sound that Dimitri misinterprets as a plea.

"What did you expect, champagne and roses?"

Laughter laces his voice. It's a rhetorical question. He knows I knew exactly what to expect. I bite my tongue and concentrate on a crack in the stone wall across from me, following its meandering path to the floor.

When my gaze falls on Vlad's body, I quickly look away.

His eyes are still open, dear God.

"All right, my love. Well done."

Dimitri leans over me, pushing my hair off my face. He kisses my cheek, his breath hot on my skin. I force myself not to react, because I know the worst is over.

If he had other plans for my body, he would've started there first.

He withdraws, smoothing his hair, and drops the whip on top of Vlad's unmoving chest. Then he watches as I carefully stand, wincing and gritting my teeth against a moan rising in the back of my throat.

Avoiding his eyes, I pull on my jeans, stopping every so often to gulp air and fight back dizziness.

I can't get the jeans buttoned with only one working hand, and I can't get my broken arm through the armhole of my T-shirt. I had to remove the sling to take the shirt off, but I'm in far too much pain now to manage to get it back on, so I just stare at it helplessly.

"Here."

Dimitri picks up the sling from the floor, loops it over my neck, then arranges my splinted arm in the cradle of fabric. He removes his suit jacket and drapes it lightly over my shoulders. I hiss in pain as the fabric settles over my burning back.

"Hush. I didn't break the skin."

He's calm now, his appetites satisfied for the moment. All in all, it's been a banner day for him. He found me, got a blow job *and* jerked himself off, and gained himself a fiancée who he immediately turned around and whipped. And he got to murder poor Vlad as a bonus.

And maybe Naz.

My heart twists. *Don't think of him now. Don't think, or you'll never be able to do this.*

Keeping my gaze lowered, I stand and wait for Dimitri to tell me what's going to happen next. I have a million questions, but asking even one would be setting a foot into a minefield. Better to let him lead the way from here and be as docile as a lamb.

Or, more accurately, a wolf in lamb's clothing.

He touches my mouth. "What are you smiling about?"

God, my stupid face. I can never keep it straight. "I'm afraid if I tell you, you'll beat me again."

He lifts my chin, forcing me to look at him. "I give you permission to speak freely."

"I . . . was wishing . . . that I could hurt you."

His lips curve up. He's amused. "Would you like that? To hurt me?"

"Yes."

I say it with so much emphasis, he chuckles.

"And how would you do it? Would you tear off my fingernails with pliers? Pour acid into my eyes? Slice off my testicles with pruning shears?"

With vehemence, I reply, "I'd set you on fire and watch you burn until you were nothing but a pile of smoking ashes, then I'd squat on top of the pile and take a shit."

For a moment, he's so stunned he doesn't react. Then he throws back his head and laughs. "My God," he says, choking with laughter. "What a little savage. Attila the Hun wasn't half as fierce!"

"Attila the Hun didn't live with you for seven years."

"Exactly." Dimitri closes his hand around my throat and draws me near. His eyes are bright with victory. His teeth are bared. "That's *exactly* right. You're my creation. My offspring. Like Athena born from the forehead of Zeus."

Though I know he's crazy, his words hold the haunting weight of prophecy. "No. I'm *not* like you—"

"You're just like me, my love. The only difference is I accept what I am, and you don't." He puts his mouth next to my ear. "You killed two of my men. If you get the opportunity, you'll kill me. You can no longer claim innocence with all the blood on your hands, especially when you don't harbor guilt for any of it."

He pulls away and smiles at my expression of horror. "Take the blinders from your eyes, Evalina. Mice don't survive in lions' dens. Only lions do."

With that, he takes my hand and leads me from the cellar.

EIGHT

Eva

We get in the Phantom and drive. Stefan follows in another car. Vlad is left to rot where he fell on the stones of the cellar.

I inhabit that black place inside my head again, which is becoming more and more comfortable. It's quiet there, and safe, a warm crawl space under the stairs of a scary old house where I can draw my knees up under my chin and hide from the monsters.

Monsters whose familiar cackles hint that I might be one of them, too.

"We're here."

I blink, drowsy, my thoughts thick and sluggish. Looking out the window into a foggy gray dawn, I see a mansion, this one not nearly as dreary as the last. White and sprawling, it sits on a hill surrounded by evergreens so tall they must have been growing for centuries.

"Here?" I watch a hawk circle lazily over the trees. It banks hard and dives like a bullet behind a hedge, then appears again, climbing back into the sky with a small wriggling bundle trapped in its talons.

"Home."

When I turn to look at Dimitri, his blue eyes are shining with excitement. He sits beside me, close but not touching, the heat of his body a constant reminder that beneath his cool, polished exterior, the pulse of an animal beats.

"I thought it wise to find a new nest for us. Considering."

Considering Tabby and Connor have his old address and would look for me there, he means. He planned it all out in advance, naturally. My capture, surrender, acceptance of his hand. I wonder if I've surprised him by how quickly I gave in.

Probably not. As long as I've known him, he's been able to anticipate my every move. My head is a crystal ball to him. He can gaze into my eyes and see my future.

He says nothing of Connor and Tabby, but they're in the slight tightness around his lips. I haven't been punished yet for them betraying him and diverting money from his bank accounts, but I suspect I will.

I can hear the dullness of my voice when I speak. "Yes. That was wise. Considering."

"You seem tired."

He's not being ironic, only observant. His gaze skips over my bruised face, my rumpled jeans, and my filthy bare feet, before traveling back up and settling on my disheveled hair. His mouth takes on a slant of disapproval.

I say, "I sheared it off on the *Silver Shadow* after Killian kidnapped me. I didn't want him to be able to use it like a leash again to hold me while he beat me."

I explain it in a matter-of-fact tone, like something that happened to someone else I've never met. It almost feels that way. A distant memory, fuzzy around the edges, already starting to fade.

"Killian?" says Dimitri, his voice edged with violence. "That's what he told you his name was?"

"Yes."

His face hardens. After a moment, he says, "He's going to pay dearly for harming you."

It's a weird species of curiosity I feel, hearing his anger that another man hit me. It must register in my face, because he asks, "What?"

"May I speak honestly again?"

"You won't be punished for being honest with me, only for disobedience."

Without thinking, I say, "That's new."

His small sigh is discontented. "No. There's a difference between insolence and honesty, rudeness and truth, rebelliousness and simple confusion about what I want."

"You once broke my arm for forgetting to make the bed."

He gazes at me, his look level and cool. "Had I instructed you to make the bed?"

I think. "Not that particular day."

"But it was a standing expectation. I hadn't changed it from the time it was given. Therefore you disobeyed, therefore you were punished."

When I stare at him with my lips parted, wrestling with the insanity of his logic, he smiles.

"Let me illustrate. Answer the following questions. Do you think I'm angry with you for sleeping with another man?"

"No," I answer instantly, "because you orchestrated it. You wanted me to have feelings for another man so you'd regain the leverage you lost when my mother died."

"Correct. But did I ever *forbid you* to sleep with another man?"

This time my answer isn't so swift. "I don't think you did specifically, but it was certainly implied."

"I wouldn't care if you fucked the entire Russian army. But only if you'd received permission from me first."

Dazed, I say faintly, "Oh. How liberated."

He lifts a shoulder. "Not really. I'd just like to watch."

"But you were going to have Vlad whip me. Why be angry with Killian but not Vlad?"

He stares at me, waiting for me to catch up.

"Because Killian didn't have permission?"

"Because he had the audacity to steal you and attempt to use you for blackmail. And yes, also because he didn't have permission to put his hands on you. You'll tell me all about him later." His voice roughens. "I want to hear what he did to cause all that bruising you had in the video he sent."

It isn't anger that roughens his voice, but excitement.

This man is an onion of evil. Peel back one stinking layer to reveal another one, even more rotten, beneath.

He misinterprets my expression as one of confusion. "Don't over-complicate it. It's very simple. Do what I tell you to do. If I don't tell you to do something, don't do it. As a perfect example: the lighter you took from Vlad. You knew it was wrong. If I'd wanted you to have one, I'd have given it to you."

Ah, but then you wouldn't have been able to orchestrate the lovely mindfuck of making me the cause of my own harm and murdering an innocent man as a bonus.

We're turning into a long, curving driveway and slowing down. The house looms ahead through the windshield, imposingly large. We pull to a stop in front of a double set of tall carved wooden doors, painted midnight black.

The color of Naz's hair.

I have to squeeze shut my eyes to keep the tears from falling.

⁓

Stefan follows glumly behind Dimitri and me as we walk through the echoing foyer and main corridor of the manor. Every surface gleams so much I want sunglasses to help with the glare.

Acres of marble, mirrors, and polished wood are only occasion-ally interrupted by a silk wall tapestry or Turkish rug. Casablanca lilies overflow from Ming vases, filling the air with that pungent, sickly-sweet funeral parlor perfume that I associate with life under Dimitri's thumb, and have therefore come to hate with a passion.

Every so often we encounter a servant in uniform. All of them stop and bow silently until we pass, never raising their gazes from the floor. As we walk, our footsteps echo hollowly off the walls.

The place has the feel of a mausoleum.

Which, in my case, I suppose it is.

"You're smiling again," notes Dimitri, stopping in front of a set of closed doors. These are white, with gold handles and matching trim.

I lift a hand to my lips, disturbed to discover he's right.

A few steps to the side and behind, Stefan stands looking at me. His gaze on me is cold and penetrating, like an interrogator's when waiting for a response in between smashing your toes with a hammer.

Dimitri turns the golden handles on the doors and pushes them open, revealing the vast suite within.

It's all white, blindingly white, from the coffered ceiling down to the glossy marble floors. All the furnishings, the statuaries and art, even the velvet draperies that frame the windows are the shade of fresh snow. Not a touch of color mars the uniformity, not even a single plant or magazine.

I look around, blinking. "How cozy and welcoming. Like an ice cave."

Dimitri sends me a sideways look, one corner of his mouth lifted. His tone turns sardonic.

"I wanted the bridal suite to reflect the purity of our love."

The bridal suite. I could vomit. "I hope your housekeeper knows how to remove bloodstains."

He eyes me, unsure if I mean mine or his.

I take a step forward, but he stops me with a curt "Wait." When I look at him, confused, he bends and picks me up in his arms.

I say to his profile, "You've got to be kidding me."

"You know I'm old fashioned."

"Sure. Like the Spanish Inquisition."

"Clever, but you'll regret that." He steps across the threshold and carries me inside.

Stefan stays just outside the doors, but his eyes track me like a pair of lasers. I try not to think of how avid his gaze was when he thought he'd be getting a front-row seat to my punishment in the cellar. I can focus on only one devil at a time.

Dimitri crosses the suite and enters the adjoining bathroom, which is as large as a hotel lobby. He sets me on my feet near a porcelain soaking tub the size of a seagoing vessel and straightens, which is when I notice how pale he's become. And there's a fine mist of perspiration on his upper lip that wasn't there moments ago.

Interesting. His physique is lean, but he's extremely strong, with the endurance of a marathon runner. That bullet must've done more damage than I guessed.

Naz's bullet.

I press a hand over my heart to stop its sudden throbbing.

"Get cleaned up. I'll send a maid to help you. You'll get a visit from the doctor later today. In the meantime, rest. You need to replenish your energy."

I look away from his suggestive smile and focus on the room. There must be something I can use as a tool or a weapon, a razor maybe. A pen. I noticed there were no bars on the windows—

"Don't bother trying to escape."

Dimitri rests his hand on the small of my back. It's a dominant gesture, one of ownership and warning despite the soft touch.

"The windows are shatterproof, and there are cameras in the walls. Your behavior determines your amount of freedom. If you displease me, you'll never leave this room."

"I understand."

He examines my expression closely, but I know my face is blank, because I feel nothing. Inside me is desolation, a barren wasteland as leached of life as the room is leached of color.

"If you need something, use the house phone." He nods at a small digital console on the wall beside the mirror. A blue touch screen awaits my command.

I need arsenic. I need a machete. I need a sharpened stake to drive straight through your unbeating heart. I turn to him with my blank face still in place. "And the wedding? When will that happen?"

He considers me in silence for a moment, his gaze lingering on my mouth. "I suppose you'll need time to select a dress."

"I . . . have a request."

He lifts his pale brows but says nothing.

"I don't want to sleep with you until then." My tone is conversational, as if I'm haggling over the price of a scarf at one of the stalls in my beloved Cozumel market and not my own desecration.

Dimitri's expression turns dangerous. "You presume too much."

"You have me now. What does a few weeks' difference make, except to whet your appetite?"

"Weeks? Oh, my love, you mistake me."

When I see the look in his eyes, my mouth goes dry.

He grabs my ass and yanks me against him, closing his other hand around my throat. He crushes his mouth to mine, biting my lip so hard he draws blood. When he pulls away, he's breathing hard and snarling.

"We'll be married in three days. If that was enough time for Christ to rise from the dead, it's enough time for us to prepare to be joined in holy matrimony."

He shoves me away and walks out, straightening his tie. The suite doors slam, a key turns in the lock, and finally—mercifully—I'm alone.

Three days. Lord help me.

I use a downy white hand towel to dab at my lip, morbidly pleased when it comes away smeared with a slash of crimson. Then I shrug off his suit jacket and kick it into a corner.

True to his word, a maid appears shortly thereafter, knocking hesitantly on the door before being let in by a glowering Stefan. The maid is young, perhaps twenty, a mousy brunette with rounded shoulders and darting eyes who flinches when I ask her name. She doesn't respond. With a lowered gaze, she gets the bathwater running and adds the contents of one of the sweet-smelling vials plucked from a mirrored tray on the counter.

Then she makes a series of incomprehensible hand motions, her fingers flashing like lightning.

"I'm sorry," I say gently. "I don't know what you mean."

She approaches me as you would a wild animal: slowly, with caution, her hands up. She glances at my unbuttoned jeans and points at the zipper.

"Oh. You want to help me out of these?"

She nods. I'm bizarrely relieved, and more than a little grateful.

"Okay. I can undo the zipper, but could you please pull down the waist?"

She nods. There's something in her manner that makes me trust her, despite her obvious wariness of me. I let her help me get undressed, then I step into the hot water, hissing in pain as it laps at the welts on my legs. It's bearable, though, and the water feels good, so I slowly lower myself until I'm seated, my splinted arm resting on the side to keep it dry.

The maid stands to one side, her eyes wide.

She was looking at my back.

"I'll bet there's medicated cream in one of those cabinets under the sink. Would you please look for me?"

She nods, moving away to the long marble sink, where she opens cabinets and drawers until she finds a tube of ointment and holds it up triumphantly.

It's no surprise to me. Dimitri always kept healing salves, bandages, and painkillers well stocked, because they were so often needed. "Good. Thank you. Maybe you could help me put that on when I get out?"

She nods again, then clasps her hands at her waist, lowering her eyes.

I want to ask her how she got here and who she is, but she's mute and I don't know sign language. Which of course would suit Dimitri's purposes perfectly. The less I can communicate with staff, the better.

I dunk my head back into the water to wet my hair, then ask the maid if there's shampoo. She selects another vial from the marble table, and I let her pour a dollop of shampoo into the palm of my hand. I scrub my scalp one-handed, then dunk again, awkwardly, trying to keep my arm elevated.

Seeing my helplessness, she holds up a finger, then disappears into the other room. She comes back quickly with an empty crystal pitcher and motions for me to sit up and tilt my head back.

Then she dunks the pitcher into the bathwater and proceeds to rinse my hair.

I close my eyes, grateful again, and also worried by how removed I feel from this. From everything that's happening to me. I don't even feel any shyness at being naked in front of this complete stranger.

If it's shock, I'm grateful for that, too, because it's better than the alternative: that I really am as resilient as Dimitri said he made me.

Because if he's right about that, he's right about everything else.

Which means I'm a monster, too.

Don't be ridiculous. Your brain is dealing with overwhelming psychological trauma. You're in denial about the reality of your situation and about me. It's natural to feel disassociated. It's a defense mechanism. There's nothing wrong with you.

"Except I'm hearing your voice inside my own head, Beastie."

I don't realize I've spoken aloud until I glance at the maid, who looks like she's mentally casting around for a cross and some holy water.

"Sorry. I'm not myself right now."

My laugh is weird and out of place. I know this because the maid slowly backs away several feet, then stands there blinking at me and swallowing.

I sigh heavily and close my eyes. "Oh God. I'm so sorry. I don't mean to scare you. I'm sure you're probably a very sweet person who had the bad luck to get a job working for a psychopath, and you've seen too much awful shit, and now here I am, looking like a punching bag and talking to myself, and you're expected to take care of me. I don't blame you for being freaked out. Just ignore me. I'm having some kind of breakdown."

To prove my point, I promptly burst into tears.

I pull my knees up and rest my forehead on them, then rock back and forth in the water as I sob, my good arm wrapped around my shins, my broken arm hurting like hell. I cry until I'm hiccuping, until I'm spiritually wrung out and physically exhausted.

Then I feel a gentle pat on my shoulder and look up.

The maid stands beside the tub, holding a fluffy white towel. On her face is a tentative smile. She points at me and makes the "OK" sign with her thumb and forefinger. I'm not sure if she's saying I'm going to be okay, or *that was a really epic crying jag, lady*, but she doesn't look afraid of me anymore, so I'm counting it as a win.

With the last of my strength, I haul myself up and step out of the tub, letting her blot water from my body as I stand there shivering from exhaustion. She rests a hand on my shoulder, and I meet her eyes.

She points at the welts on my back, her gaze questioning.

"Dimitri had a little fun with me earlier."

She nods slowly, her eyes hardening. Then she points at her mouth.

"I don't understand."

She points at my back, then at her mouth.

"Are you saying Dimitri is the reason you don't speak?"

When she nods, my stomach does a slow roll.

"Oh God. I'm afraid to ask."

I don't have to, though, because she simply shows me what Dimitri did by opening her mouth.

The queasiness turns to a hot rush of bile up my throat as I stare at the mutilated stub of flesh that is the remains of her tongue.

NINE

Naz

"Don't fuck this up."

"I'm not going to fuck anything up."

"You have to be extremely careful."

"You think I don't know that?"

"He could have the place booby-trapped. He could have scouts, cameras, who knows what. It could all be a setup."

Killian rolls his eyes. "Stop fretting. You're like an old woman."

I'm still lying on the cot, all my holes stitched, now hooked up to IV antibiotics, watching Killian gear up and get ready to go to the last location of Eva's GPS, and feeling like an absolute failure of a man because he's going in my place.

My woman. My responsibility. Period.

Except for the bullet hole bullshit, which is really pissing me off.

"I need a phone."

"Doc will give you whatever you need."

Killian jerks his chin toward Doc, who's on the other side of the warehouse, rummaging through a big stainless-steel refrigerator. He said sewing me up gave him a craving for a burger, which is all kinds of fucking strange, but I was too preoccupied with Killian and his mission to get into it.

Not that I really wanna know, anyway.

"You got backup?"

Killian makes a face at me, like I'm being silly because he's way too good to need backup. That pisses me off, too.

"I need details. This is driving me nuts."

"You were already nuts, mate."

"Killian. Please."

He stops, arrested by the tone of my voice, and by the word *please*, which I'm sure I've never uttered before in his presence.

My voice rough, I say, "She's my life. She's my whole life."

After staring at my expression for a moment, he zips up his flak jacket and slings a pack over his shoulders. He changed out of his suit faster than Clark Kent changes in a phone booth, and now he's in full tactical gear and a pair of scuffed combat boots, which are annoyingly big.

He probably stuffs socks into the toes.

He says, "So when I bring her back in one piece, you'll owe me."

Then he's gone, leaving me spitting obscenities after him.

From across the warehouse, Doc calls out, "You want a burger, man? I make a mean bacon cheeseburger with all the trimmings."

I holler, "I don't want a fucking hamburger! I want a fucking phone!"

"You want a phone, but what you *need* is a chill pill, dude." He ambles over to the desk where the computers are, munching on a stalk of celery. "If anybody can get your girl back, it's that man who just left. He's legendary."

I swear a blood vessel in my brain is about to burst. "So he keeps telling me."

From a drawer of the desk, Doc removes a black cell phone. He turns it on, presses a few buttons, then brings it over to me.

"Is this secure?"

"Duh."

I take it from him and start dialing Connor's number. "I suppose if I asked you about Killian, you wouldn't tell me anything."

"Not at all. Ask away."

He's so nonchalant and the answer is so unexpected, I stop in the middle of dialing and look up.

"Okay. Who is he?"

"You mean who is he *really*? I have no clue, man. I don't even know if Killian is his real name."

I deadpan, "Thanks. That's super helpful. So glad we had this heart-to-heart."

"I'm just telling you the truth. He operates on a need-to-know basis, and pretty much everything about him is do-not-need-to-know."

"How'd you meet him?"

"I was freelancing for Uncle Sam—"

"You're American?"

"Nope."

We stare at each other. "I think the follow-up question is pretty obvious."

He says, "What does my nationality have to do with anything? Governments all over the world hire noncitizens for black ops. The US just happens to have a really fat budget for back-channel jobs, so I work with them most often."

"So you're a spy."

"First and foremost, I'm a doctor. I just go where the work takes me. And in Killian's case, it was a job in Pakistan. I met him right before he tipped off the CIA to bin Laden's location—"

"Wait." I prop myself up on my elbows, prickling with disbelief. "You're telling me *Killian* was responsible for taking down bin Laden?"

"No, man," he says, eyes glinting with mischief. "SEAL Team Six took down bin Laden. Killian just told them where he was hiding."

"Bullshit. He made that up."

Doc lifts his hands. "I'm only saying, I overheard the man make a phone call and give somebody an address to a compound in Abbottabad, and not even an hour later, bin Laden was dead at a compound at that address in Abbottabad. You do the math."

"If you overheard him, he *wanted* you to overhear him! He was probably talking to a dial tone!"

"Nah, there've been way too many other things like that. He's the real deal. Anyway, he and I got friendly after I saved his brother's leg. Stepped on an antipersonnel mine over in Rawalpindi—"

"What? Killian has a *brother*?"

"A twin, yeah. He's in the biz, too."

We stare at each other. Doc munches on his celery. I say, "A *twin*. This just keeps getting better and better."

"They look exactly alike. Kinda creepy, actually. Same tattoos and everything."

"That is creepy."

"Tell me about it. There've been a few times I wasn't sure which one of them I was talking to."

"What's the brother's name?"

"Liam."

"Do you know their last name?"

He scoffs. "Sure. You want Killian's social security number and date of birth, too? He gave me a file with all his personal info in it."

"God, I really hate that guy."

"He's really great once you get to know him."

I flop back down onto the cot and exhale a heavy breath. "He keeps telling me that, too."

"Give him a chance. He'll grow on you."

"Right. Like mold. What else can you tell me about him?"

Doc thinks for a minute, finishes the stalk of celery, and wipes his mouth with the back of his hand. "He hates disco music."

"Oh, for fuck's sake."

"All I know, man, is the guy is a ghost. He's the best at what he does, and he's a ghost. When he wants me for a job, he calls me. If I can make it, I come. He pays me in cash, I do the job, we don't chat about our childhood traumas. I happened to be in town for a convention, so you got lucky and got me instead of whatever quack he could rustle up on short notice."

"A convention?"

He shrugs. "EuroSciCon is putting on World Pathology Week. I'm big into continuing education."

I close my eyes and mutter, "I can't believe this shit." Then I open my eyes and finish dialing Connor's number.

"We done with sharing time?" asks Doc, grinning.

"Go away."

He ambles off back toward the refrigerator and the long stainless-steel table that makes up the kitchen portion of the warehouse, then gets busy assembling his meal.

The line is answered on the first ring. Into the heavy silence, I say, "Connor. It's Naz."

"Jesus Christ." A relieved sigh comes over the phone. "We on a secure line?"

"Yeah."

"Günter said you were picked up by an ambulance, but you never showed up at a hospital. I thought one of Dimitri's guys nabbed you and dumped you in a ditch."

"I got picked up by Killian. I'm at his safe house somewhere in the city now."

"Killian?"

"Trust me, I was just as surprised as you are."

Connor grunts. "The man's big into rescues."

"If you say we should hire him, I'll quit."

"Any idea where the safe house is?"

"None. I'm full of holes and nonoperational, but stable enough." I give him a quick rundown of what happened, filling him in on where Killian went and what Doc told me about him and his brother.

"Twins. Interesting."

"More like irritating."

"Tabby might be able to use it to dig up something on him, though. I mean, them. Talk to me about your condition."

"Doc says it's not life-threatening, but I'm feeling pretty hairy. I'll be down for at least a few days."

"Copy that. How soon will you be ready for exfil?"

"No exfil. I'm staying put until Killian gets back."

Connor's pause is weighted. "You think you can trust him?"

"Not as far as I could throw him. But I need to be right here if he comes back with Eva."

"And if he comes back without her?"

My lungs start to ache again. "I'll deal with that then."

"Your call, brother."

"Has Tabby picked up any new intel about Dimitri?"

"No chatter on the ground yet, but we've been watching his estate via satellite. Far as we can tell, nobody's come or gone. Looks real quiet. Unless they've hacked the sat."

"He would've anticipated we'd be watching. He's too smart to take Eva somewhere we already know. See if Tabby can find out if he's bought any new properties, signed any new leases. There's gotta be a paper trail somewhere."

"She's already on it, brother."

Of course she is. God bless her. "That's awesome. Thank you."

His voice drops. "We're watchin' all the hospitals in the country, too. Just in case."

Staring at the ceiling, I blow out a hard breath.

"Can I call you back on this line, or is it a burner?"

I shout across the warehouse, "Doc! Can I keep this phone?"

"Sure, man. It's all yours."

I navigate to apps and pull up the phone's number from the SIM card, then read it off to Connor.

"Copy that. Gimme the coordinates where Killian went, and I'll see what we can get on our end. Address, sat view, whatever's available."

When I don't respond, Connor prompts, "You still there?"

"Yeah."

After a moment, Connor guesses the reason for my continued silence. "He didn't give you the coordinates, did he?"

"No."

"Any way you can get 'em?"

I look over at the computer screens. They're all dark.

Son of a bitch.

I shout over to Doc, "Can you get me the coordinates where Killian went?"

He looks up from the bowl of raw hamburger meat he's mixing together with his hands. "Sure, I'll just pull those right outta my ass, dude." Shaking his head and chuckling, he goes back to mixing.

"Fuck."

Connor says, "I'll take that as a no."

My heart starts to pound. *What if he doesn't come back? What if he finds Eva but never comes back with her? She doesn't even know if I'm alive. He could tell her a million different stories, get her to go with him, they could disappear—*

"I can hear your mind spinning, brother. Take a deep breath."

I growl, "We have to find out who this fucker is!"

"We will. In the meantime, keep your head in the game and stay focused. Call me if you get anything new, and see if you can find out your location. I'd like to get eyes on that safe house."

I hear the concern in his voice. Obviously, neither one of us trusts Killian.

"I'll holler at you when I have something."

"Keep frosty till then, brother."

"Will do. You too."

Never one for long goodbyes—or even short ones—Connor disconnects.

Now the only thing left for me to do is wait.

And obsess over what Killian said before he left, which at the time seemed strange but now seems downright sinister.

"Some people are very skilled at playing two sides against each other without either side ever knowing what's going on."

Who the hell is he working for?

TEN

Eva

A different doctor than the one who set my arm on the plane comes to see me. He's tall, gray haired, and thin as a whip, and he breathes garlic fumes into my face as he frowns over the stitches in my cheek. He gives my arm a cursory examination, nods in satisfaction, then rewraps the splint and tells me there's nothing more he can do until the swelling goes down.

"Ice it. I'll come back to see you tomorrow. Take one of these every three to four hours for the pain."

He hands me an unmarked amber bottle of pills and leaves.

As soon as he's gone, I pretend to swallow one of the pills, in case Dimitri's watching. Then I cough it out into my palm and drop it into the toilet when I pee.

The mute maid left after applying a thin layer of antibiotic cream to my back and legs after my bath. She hasn't returned since. I'm still not over the shock of seeing that mangled piece of flesh in her mouth. I have the horrifying thought that maybe all the servants in the manor are mute as well, but I decide it would be too much, even for Dimitri, to carve out the tongues of an entire staff of domestic workers.

I hope.

After I explore the room, the night tables and dresser drawers, and the enormous closet—finding nothing I could use to stab a man in the jugular—I go back into the bathroom and tap the console on the wall.

A woman's pleasant, professional voice immediately answers in Russian. *"Da, gospozha?"*

She has a hint of a German accent in her speech, so I answer in German. I need to make all the friends I can get here at Dr. Frankenstein's castle. "Good morning. I'm Evalina, and I'm starving. Will you please send in some food?"

After a surprised beat of silence, she answers back in German, her tone warm. "Yes, madam. Is there anything in particular you'd like?"

"Whatever's easiest for you . . ."

"Astrid," she supplies into my pause.

"Astrid. What a lovely name. Well, whatever you have that you don't have to go to too much trouble for would be wonderful, Astrid. Thank you."

"Ah . . . you're welcome, madam."

My politeness is taking her aback. I suppose she isn't used to such niceties from the lord of the manor.

"Anything to drink?"

I almost say rum, but I remind myself alcohol wouldn't be good for any baby Beastie I might have on board. "Water, I suppose. Or vegetable juice if you have it. But you should have a cocktail on me, Astrid. I'm sure you deserve it."

I wish the console had a video camera. I'd love to see her expression. Her surprised silences are getting longer and longer.

"I . . . don't believe I'm allowed, madam. But . . . thank you."

"You're welcome. Also if you'd please send a bucket of ice, I'd appreciate it very much."

I disconnect, my limbs heavy with fatigue. How long has it been since I slept? I don't know. Time has become elastic. It could be a day or a hundred years since I last felt Naz's skin on mine. Since my heart took its last real beat.

I wander over to the window and stand looking at the lawn rolling away into mist. Dark figures prowl around the edges. Armed guards, hunting for trespassers through the trees.

When the food arrives, brought on a rolling table covered with a linen cloth and delivered by the mute maid, my stomach turns at the smell. I have to force myself to sit, chew, and swallow, knowing Dimitri's eyes are in the walls.

When I can't eat any more, I gather a fistful of ice into the middle of a linen napkin, fold the corners together, and press it against my cheek until I can't stand the cold, then switch it to my arm. I take turns going back and forth between them until all the ice is melted.

Then I curl into a ball on top of the silk duvet on the king-size bed and drop into a dreamless sleep.

When I wake, it's dark outside. The cart of food is gone and so is the nausea. My arm throbs so badly I'm tempted to take one of the painkillers, but I only pretend to instead. I wait, pacing and tense, for something to happen, for Dimitri to arrive and my debasement to begin, but he doesn't come.

No one comes.

I'm left alone until the morning, when the garlicky doctor visits again. He must brush his teeth with the stuff.

"Much better," he says after unwrapping the splint from my arm.

I don't know how he can tell. All I see is black-and-blue skin, shiny and swollen like an overripe plum. "Do I need surgery?"

When he shakes his head, my heart sinks.

"Your fingers are working. The swelling is going down. I'll put a cast on it tomorrow."

No trip to the hospital, then. No chance to get near an unattended phone.

On his way out the door, I catch a glimpse of Stefan, watching me with those eyes of his, sharp as a cat's. The dark cloud over his face gives me pause.

He closes the door and locks it. I hurry over to press my ear against the wood, my heartbeat picking up, my blood singing with a strange intuition.

I hear male voices, murmuring. Indistinct. Then the doctor, sounding agitated.

"I told you, I haven't examined him. He uses another physician. I know nothing."

Him? Does he mean Dimitri?

More murmuring. Then the sound of footsteps echoing over the marble floor, fading into the distance.

I turn away from the door, filled with anxiousness but trying to appear calm. I don't wring my hands or pace again. I simply walk into the closet and select the most comfortable clothing I can find, a silk sheath the shimmering turquoise of a mermaid's tail. I select a bra and panties from the dresser drawers, struggling to get the bra on with only one operational arm but finally managing it, then put on the dress. It's easy to pull over my head, supple and light, with no buttons or zippers for swollen fingers to fumble with. A pair of black silk slippers completes the look.

The closet is bursting with couture in every rainbow color, all of it in my size. A gift from my intended.

God, I wish I had a can of petrol and a match. I'd love to watch all of it burn.

Into the console on the bathroom wall, I say, "I'd like to go for a walk outside."

I say it with authority, as if there's no question I'll be allowed. As if I'm not a wounded bird trapped in this pretty cage.

Either my confidence works or this wasn't forbidden in the first place, because Astrid answers with a cheerful "Of course, madam."

Good. Let's get a better look at my prison. Let's see where the bars are bent.

Stefan unlocks the door and swings it open, allowing me to step into the hallway. The *freezing* hallway. Corpses could be kept fresh in this temperature for months.

When I shiver, running a hand up my bare arm, he shrugs out of his suit jacket—stopping to stick his rifle between his thighs—and settles it over my shoulders without a word. It's warm and scented of him: pine needles and cigarette smoke, a cheap, spicy cologne.

"Thank you."

He inclines his head, then takes up his rifle again and levels me with a look, dark and inscrutable. "This way."

We don't take the same route we came in yesterday, through the main entry and the midnight-black doors. Instead, he leads me through a series of rooms and corridors, winding and seemingly endless, until we emerge through a windowless door onto a plain paved driveway at the back of the property.

I look around, frowning.

"Servants' entrance," he says.

The driveway opens to a narrow unpaved road that leads south through the trees. On either side is meadow. The house is behind, elevated on a knoll overlooking the driveway but set back far enough that if you were inside looking out through a window, you couldn't see where I'm standing.

The silence would be deafening, except for the whispering of the wind through the tips of the trees.

I turn and face Stefan. "If you're going to shoot me, let's get it over with. I'm cold."

He knits his brows, gazing at me as if I'm a riddle he can't quite solve. "Why did you do it?"

"Do what?"

"Offer to take Vlad's punishment."

His question catches me completely off guard. Not only by the gentle tone in which it was spoken—a tone at odds with everything I've seen of him so far—but because it's forbidden. I'm sure he's aware that if I told Dimitri about this, he'd be dead. Or at least wishing he were.

So whatever's behind his curiosity, it's very important. It's also important that I tell him the truth.

"Because he didn't do anything wrong except step in the middle of an old, ugly game between me and Dimitri."

He examines my face, his frown deepening. "What are you to him?"

I think about that for a moment as the mist plays around the hem of my dress. "A challenge, I think. Predators are happiest when the hunt isn't easy."

He shakes his head, dissatisfied with my answer. "I've seen him with other girls. You're different. It's like he's . . . addicted. Obsessed."

"Because of all the women I've ever had, only you have proven to be unbreakable."

I smother the memory of Dimitri's words. The logic of a monster wouldn't make sense to a regular man. It takes me a moment to come up with something that might.

"I suppose it's because I know how his mind works."

Stefan's confusion is obvious. He's trying to work out our relationship. I think I'll help him along.

"I met him when I was twenty. I was naive. A child. But not for long. He held me captive, me and my mother both, and did whatever he wanted to us. When she died, I escaped." My smile is grim. "But not for long. He has me back now. He intends to marry me. A terrible decision, really, because as soon as I get the chance, I'm going to kill him."

Stefan stares at me in silence, but I glimpse a whirlwind behind his eyes. There's something important here I need to tease out.

I say gently, "It's all right if you have to tell him I said that. I understand your position, where your loyalty lies."

He huffs out a breath and looks away. "You don't know anything about my loyalties."

The soldier has defected, but the general doesn't yet know. It's in every taut line of his body, every telling tic on his face. But there's something else beneath his tension, a darker, more painful emotion that has him grinding his jaw and white-knuckling his weapon as he stands there staring into the distance.

Goose bumps erupt all over my arms. I say, "Vlad."

Without looking at me, he nods.

"He was . . . your friend? Brother?"

His Adam's apple bobs. A quick shake of his head, and I know.

His lover.

I breathe, "Oh, Stefan. I'm so sorry."

He speaks through a clenched jaw. "I was the one who got him the job. It was a mistake. He wasn't cut out for this kind of work. He was too . . ." He pauses to swallow. "He didn't know about my feelings. No one knows. I don't even know why I'm telling you."

Our eyes meet. That little jolt of recognition.

"Yes, you do."

It hangs there between us, unspoken: *because you want to kill Dimitri, too.*

Nothing more is said. I make a show of walking the grounds, giving Stefan his coat back before we come in sight of the house. He trails behind me at a respectable distance as I meander through manicured gardens, everything glimmering with mist. When my slippers are soaked and I can no longer bear the cold, I ask Stefan to take me back inside.

We go through the front door this time, arriving as a large white van is pulling into the driveway. A pair of the armed guards I saw lurking around earlier approach the van, and one of them taps on the driver's window with his rifle. Stefan and I go into the house before I can hear what's happening.

"Enjoy your walk?"

I jump at the sound of Dimitri's voice and whirl around. He's sitting in a wingback chair in the drawing room, dressed in black silk, shoes polished, cuff links gleaming, not a hair out of place. The gold-and-onyx signet ring on his pinkie winks in the light.

He slides a look at Stefan, his lips lifting, then glances back at me. *Careful now, Eva. Don't blink.*

I answer coolly, "If your dog wasn't sniffing so closely at my heels, I would have."

"Hmm."

He tilts his head back and examines me for a moment from under half-lowered lids. Stefan stands silent and still, his face blank, his demeanor untroubled.

He's much better at this than Vlad was.

His gaze on me unflinching, Dimitri lifts his hand and makes a "come" motion with his index finger.

I obey without hesitation but don't hurry. He watches the dress move around my hips as I walk. When I'm a foot away, he reaches out and grabs my wrist, then yanks me down into his lap.

He bites me on the shoulder, sliding his hand up my thigh.

I stiffen and suck in a breath.

What a stupid mistake this dress was. A slip of a thing, so easy to get into but so utterly easy to rip off. I should've wound myself up in corsets and packing tape.

"Steady, my love," murmurs Dimitri, nuzzling my neck as I instinctively recoil. "Or I'll think you don't like me touching you."

His soft chuckle makes my flesh crawl. He brutally pinches the tender flesh of my inner thigh, chuckling again when I gasp in pain, squeezing my legs together.

Stefan gazes at us impassively, his expression almost bored. But there's a spark of something in his eyes that wasn't there before. A flash of anger, there then quickly smothered.

"Excuse me, sir."

Dimitri looks up at the guard standing in the corridor. He's tall and broad shouldered, with close-cropped dark hair and a nose that's been broken more than once. "The dressmaker is here."

"Ah!" Dimitri brightens. "Bring him in."

Dressmaker? That sinking feeling is my stomach.

The guard shows in an old man with gnarled hands and a shock of white hair. Though bent and limping, he has a proud bearing. His suit is fine-quality navy pinstripe. His bow tie and silk pocket square are both red.

He's accompanied by another man, much younger, wearing a rumpled beige cardigan and black bifocal glasses on the bridge of his large nose. A tape measure dangles from around his neck. An assistant.

They bow. The old man murmurs a deferential greeting.

"Come in, Alek. Welcome."

The old man gestures to his companion. "My son, Tolya."

The son bows again. He's nervous, perspiring, pushing his glasses up his nose but staring at the floor. Obviously his father has warned him about their patron.

The two of them have my eternal gratitude, because Dimitri is distracted.

"You've brought samples?"

Alek nods.

"Good. Let's begin. Evalina, get undressed."

Alek, Tolya, Stefan, and the guard all look at me.

Heat floods my face.

I understand that my humiliation is part of it, that Dimitri arranged this not only as another test of obedience but also as one of the little degradations he so enjoys. If I'm to be successful in my drive to earn his trust, I must do as he commands.

But it would be easier to swallow a flaming sword than to force my frozen limbs to move.

Dimitri waits, smiling blandly, staring into my eyes.

My choice is clear. Obey, or pay.

Either way, he wins.

This battle, I remind myself, but not the war.

I stand and face Tolya and Alek. My fingers shaking, I untie the sling around my neck, let the piece of fabric fall to the floor, and slip the dress off my shoulders. It pools around my waist. I have to push it over my hips, one at a time, then let it slide down my legs until it crumples into a puddle around my ankles. The entire process takes an eternity.

Then I stand there in my bra and panties, cradling my arms against my chest, miserable but resigned. The sooner this is over with, the better.

The room is utterly silent for a moment, until Dimitri says to Alek, "Should she take off her underwear, too? Would that make for a better fitting?"

It's polite and deadly. The heat in my cheeks flames hotter. It becomes impossible to breathe.

A supreme professional, Alek shakes his head. "For the fit, it's best if she wears the undergarments she'll be wearing the day of the ceremony."

Oh, thank God. Not complete humiliation, then.

Except I've forgotten who I'm dealing with.

Adjusting his cuff links, Dimitri says casually, "In that case, she should take off everything. She'll be nude under her gown on our wedding day." He looks at me, his eyes glittering, a smile dancing around the edges of his mouth.

I feel sorry for Tolya, who looks mortified. He's probably a good boy. Goes to church. Loves his mother. Alek is too smart to show his reaction one way or another, and merely waits. Stefan waits, too, his face blank, the earlier flash of anger controlled.

The other guard is grinning.

"You two." I jerk my chin at Stefan and the grinning guard. "Get out."

Stefan is smart. He doesn't obey my instruction, but looks to Dimitri instead.

I say to Dimitri, "It's up to you, of course, but it doesn't seem wise to let them stay." I turn my head and meet his gaze. "Unless you think they'll keep their hands to themselves when you're not around."

"Perhaps I gave them permission," he drawls.

He's poking at me with a stick, trying to get a reaction. I won't give him one. "You'd let the help have sex with your wife?"

"You're not my wife yet."

"But I will be soon. And then all your men can say they work for a cuckold. Doesn't seem as if that would engender the utmost respect."

Thrust. Parry. Feint. Around and around we go, until infinity.

Unfortunately, his rapier is always sharper than mine.

Gazing at me steadily, he says, "If you're not naked within the next ten seconds, I'll call in the entire staff and beat you bloody in front of them all, and then I'll fuck you in front of them all, and they'll have much more to talk about than me being a cuckold. Your choice."

His smile is angelic.

Everyone in the room holds their breath.

My cheeks burning, I reach behind my back and unhook my bra.

ELEVEN

Eva

I keep telling myself I've suffered far worse things, but with every new male guard, houseboy, and cook who wanders past the drawing room as I'm being measured in the nude, my shame grows.

Along with it grows my fury.

Naz would never have allowed something like this. He'd die to protect my honor. If another man dared to look at me undressed, he'd make sure it would be a long time before he could look at anything else again.

But of course this isn't love. This is ownership. This is a show of power, so that everyone knows I'm a piece of property. Dimitri's toy to do with as he likes.

An equal, my ass.

After a pimply servant makes his third pass by the room, gawking, I can no longer hold my tongue. Over Tolya's head—he's bent down, the tape measure around my waist as he fumbles with it with shaking fingers—I say to Dimitri, "There's some honesty headed your way, if you're in the mood to hear it."

He lights a cigar before he responds. He takes his time with it, tranquilly cutting the tip with a tiny pair of folding scissors unfolded from the bottom of his silver lighter, then lighting up and puffing. He deposits the snipped piece of tobacco into a crystal ashtray on the small table beside his chair, dusts off his fingers, and blows a perfect ring of smoke through his lips.

"My anticipation knows no bounds."

He's laughing at me. Mocking me. I wonder if he knows how much I'd like to shred his eyeballs with the tiny pair of scissors.

Tolya murmurs my waist measurement to his father, who jots it down on a small pad. He moves on to my hips, his face the color of a beet.

"If I'm to be your wife, you're undermining my position. None of these men will ever show me respect after this."

"You're not the one they need to respect."

Poor Vlad found that out the hard way. I wonder if the rest of the staff knows what happened to him. Though he might be devastated, Stefan seems too cagey to open his mouth and risk Dimitri's displeasure.

"Is that why you killed Vlad?"

Tolya drops his measuring tape. The pimply servant blanches and turns around, hurrying back the way he came. Hopefully to spread the news that Vlad is dead.

I'm guessing he was well liked. Perhaps Stefan wasn't the only one with a crush. Maybe there will be a mutiny . . .

Dimitri chuckles. "Look at those wheels turning. I enjoy seeing you like this."

"Humiliated?"

"Strategizing."

Our gazes meet and hold. He puffs on his cigar, a lion lazing in his den, belly full with a fresh kill, licking blood off his chops.

The urge to drive my thumbs into his eye sockets is nearly overpowering. I hate him so much he should drop dead from the sheer electrical force of it leaving my body, like being struck by a bolt of lightning.

As Tolya picks up his tape and measures the length of my leg from hip to ankle, his fingers icy against my bare skin, Dimitri turns philosophical. "Love and hate are two different sides of the same coin, Evalina. Your hate binds you to me just as much as your love did to your mother. Or Nasir."

I look away, unnerved that he read my thoughts and despising the sound of Naz's name on his lips. I can't bear to hear it.

Tolya gives a measurement to his father, who dutifully jots it down. Then Tolya rises, nervously licking his lips. He stutters, "E-excuse me please, madam, b-but I . . . may I . . ."

He gestures toward my breasts. His ears are scarlet.

"No, you may not. Thirty-six."

He glances at Dimitri, who waves his cigar, smirking and thoroughly enjoying himself. "As she says. Bring in the gowns."

I don't know who's more relieved, me or Tolya, who exhales and wipes his forehead with the back of his hand before scurrying out the door, tape measure flying. His father follows.

As we wait for the dresses to be brought in, Dimitri transfers his cigar to his other hand, then reaches out and trails a finger down my spine. I suppress a flinch and bite my lip.

"You found the cream for your welts," he says, tracing a line across my back.

"Yes. The maid helped me."

"Your skin always marks so nicely. It will be even better when the tan fades. You've spent too much time in the sun." His finger drifts down to the upper curve of my bottom, then lingers on my tailbone, tracing a figure eight. He murmurs to himself, "My initials would be perfect tattooed here. No—branded."

Horrified at the prospect, I swallow and draw a shaky breath.

Across the room, Stefan watches, his face darkening.

Standing next to him, the guard with the broken nose has a visible erection.

I force myself to breathe and relax my muscles. Despite Dimitri's offhand remark about giving his men permission to have me, I don't believe this is a prelude to gang rape. He's never allowed anyone in his employ to touch me, or offered me to a business associate during one of those many past meetings where a variety of girls were presented as gifts.

On the threat of beating me and bending me over in front of the staff, however, I have no doubt.

Dimitri slaps my bottom, making me jump. "Look at me."

When I do, he demands, "Tell me what you were just thinking."

"You don't share me."

His gaze bores into mine. "Not yet, I haven't."

After a moment, I decide to take a risk. I lower my gaze to the floor and say quietly, "I'm grateful that you don't."

I'm surprised to hear him laugh. I look up at him again, taken aback. "I was being honest."

"You were being calculated."

He's not angry. If anything, he seems pleased. "And you like that because . . . ?"

He cups my bottom and squeezes, sinking his fingers into my flesh. "The same reason a gardener likes watching the seeds he plants bloom into flowers."

A flash of anger tightens my stomach. Lord save me from his stupid creation analogies. "I'm not a thing you made."

His smile sours. "Don't be boring. You're a queen. Wear your crown proudly."

Tolya and Alek return with the dresses, pulling them in on rolling garment racks, a profusion of silk, tulle, chiffon, and seed pearls, everything the purest snowy white.

"Such a long face," notes Dimitri, puffing on his cigar. "The gowns don't please you?"

I scowl at the sea of frothy confections being assembled around me. It isn't the color I hate, but the thought of what they symbolize: a legalized union with this creature sitting beside me, this monster posing as a man with his elegant manners and expensive suit.

If I marry him and then kill him, I'll be a widow. A black widow. A murderer times three. I'll be . . .

Oh my God. If I'm pregnant and we marry, my child will be his heir.

Dimitri picks up a folded newspaper from the table next to his chair and flips it open over his knee. As more racks are rolled in by a handful of guards, he says, "Or perhaps you'd prefer something more appropriate for a woman in mourning? Black, I suppose?"

There's a triumphant tone in his voice that makes me look at him sharply.

He's reading an article, a smile stretching his lips wide. When he finishes, he offers it over without a word.

A dark premonition strikes a chord of terror deep in my heart. I stare at the newspaper, no longer aware of the room or the gowns or my exposed flesh, no longer caring about the state of my humiliation.

Dimitri turns his head and looks at me, and I know. His smile is so vicious, I already know.

I whisper, *"No."*

"Shall I read it to you? It's quite short. There's a picture, too."

All the tiny hairs on my body standing on end and my heart racing like mad, I glance down at the newspaper.

At the story's headline: American One of Ten Killed in Violent Shoot-Out.

At the picture of Naz's face.

Dimitri tosses the paper back onto the table and takes a puff of his cigar. "You thought I was lying, didn't you? Ouch. That must really hurt."

Shattering into a thousand jagged pieces, I sink to my knees with the sound of his soft laughter ringing in my ears.

It takes both Stefan and Tolya to get me standing again, though I'm not able to remain that way for long.

Stefan is tasked with holding me up while Tolya helps me in and out of dress after dress. Patient as a saint, his gaze lowered, he gently takes my feet one by one and lifts them into the opening of another rustling skirt, sets my foot on the floor, waits until Stefan balances me, then does the same routine with the other foot and pulls the skirt up my legs.

Buttons are pushed through buttonholes. Snaps are snapped. Silk ties are tied.

All the while I remain entombed in a body that now serves as a crypt for my heart.

My devastation is so total I'm unable to cry. The proof of Naz's death has hit me like an atom bomb, flattening everything inside with a scalding flash of heat and a powerful shock wave of pressure. I'm a wasteland of poison gas and smoking cinders, howling, acid winds.

He's gone. My love is gone. My kind, soulful, beautiful man . . .

Gone.

And I'm in ruin.

"This one is pretty," says Dimitri, gesturing at me with his cigar.

I'm swathed in yards of crepe and French lace. A funeral shroud. I stare at nothing, unable to see.

Naz.

"It's very flattering to her figure," agrees Alek. "That slender waist."

"All right. We'll take it."

"Very good. A veil to match, sir?"

"If you recommend it."

"I do."

Dimitri waves a hand. It's done.

Naz.

Tolya and Stefan share a look I don't bother to interpret, then the two of them assist me out of the sample dress. I no longer care about my nudity or even notice it. I can't feel the air on my skin. The room and everyone in it is far away, beyond the howling winds and poisonous gases.

Another guard enters the room. As faceless and interchangeable as all the others. "Sir, your physician is here."

"Show him in."

The guard leaves. Dimitri stands—

And wobbles.

He grips Stefan's shoulder to steady himself, then straightens his tie. He smooths a hand over his hair. When the doctor enters the room, Dimitri drops his hand from Stefan's shoulder and welcomes him with an untroubled voice.

"Stefan, see Evalina to the bridal suite."

He leaves, ushering the doctor down the corridor with a sure step.

He doesn't look back. If he did, he'd see Stefan's look. The sharp, cat-eyed look, the one that doesn't miss anything.

Dimitri didn't come to me last night.

The wobble and the thought are connected, but I'm too dead to care.

With Dimitri gone, Stefan takes over. He issues a curt command for the other guards to remove the rolling dress racks to the truck outside, which is obeyed without question. Alek and Tolya follow, giving Stefan a wide berth.

I sense the hierarchy of things, the undercurrents of power.

The room emptied, Stefan snatches my turquoise sheath from the floor and tries to find the hem. It's slithering liquid in his hands. He throws it aside, irritated, and removes his jacket. He slings it over my shoulders and doesn't bother asking if I can walk.

The answer must be more than obvious.

He picks me up and carries me from the room.

As he strides down the empty corridor, he says through barely moving lips, "He's injured."

"Shot," I answer, finding the right word through the desolation in my head.

"Your doing?"

Naz. I shake my head, a sob sticking in my throat.

"Why doesn't he go to the hospital?"

"Paranoia. Enemies everywhere. And he thinks he's invincible. A god."

We turn a corner, encountering a maid dusting a carved sideboard. She scurries out of our way. When she's gone, Stefan murmurs, "He's in trouble with Pakhan. Overstepping boundaries. Losing money. Attracting attention."

Pakhan is the boss in the Russian Bratva. The godfather who controls everything. Dimitri is extremely powerful and connected, but there's only one man in all of Russia who answers to no one, and it isn't him.

This bit of information tells me that Stefan has not only defected from Dimitri's side, he's actively working against him. Not only that, but he's decided to trust me.

"Does Pakhan know about the nuke?"

There is the slightest falter in his step before he recovers. "Nuke?"

"Dimitri made a deal with the president of Venezuela to send him a UR-100 warhead."

"Are you positive?"

"Yes."

"Do you have proof?"

"No. But I know someone who does."

"Give me the name."

I close my eyes and rest my head on his broad shoulder, a weight like a thousand pounds of stones crushing my chest. "I'll do you one better," I whisper. "I'll give you his phone number, too."

TWELVE

NAZ

"I look like shit."

"Really? I think you look good."

"I hate that picture. It's my passport picture. I look constipated."

Leaning over me and gazing at the newspaper in my hand, Doc shrugs. "I never look that good when I'm constipated."

The way he says it makes me think he owns a lot of laxatives. Probably due to all the meat he eats. In the past day, he's made himself four bacon cheeseburgers, as many roast beef sandwiches, steak and eggs, double-stuffed carnitas burritos, and several large cans of beef stew. Right now he's polishing off a bag of turkey jerky, and he shakes the bag in my face.

"Want some?"

"I'm not hungry."

"You gotta eat, man. You can't go on a hunger strike—it won't help you heal. And you gotta hydrate. Here." He hands me a bottle of water.

I'm propped up on pillows on a battered brown leather sofa that looks as if it were reclaimed from the dump. There's a small living area set up next to the kitchen, with a bed, nightstand, bookcase, and the dumpy sofa. A scarred wooden coffee table holds a silver cigar ashtray and a biography of the seventies movie star Steve McQueen.

It's in French, just to be doubly annoying. That bastard Killian probably speaks a bunch of foreign languages. All with a perfect accent, no doubt.

I toss the newspaper with the article of my demise onto the coffee table. At least the Germans were good for one thing. Hopefully, wherever he is, Dimitri sees it. "How long has Killian been gone?"

"Fifteen minutes longer than the last time you asked me."

"Why doesn't he call? It's been more than twenty-four hours!"

"Because he doesn't have anything yet. When he has something, he'll call."

I stare with intense loathing at the IV catheter stuck into the vein on the back of my hand. "When can you take this off?"

"For the fourth time, when the bag of antibiotics is empty."

"There's something wrong with the drip. It's taking forever."

Doc ambles over to the bed, flops down on it, threads his hands behind his head on the pillow, and crosses his feet. "There's nothing wrong with the drip, man. Chill."

Chill. As if I fucking could.

My mind is a horror movie fest, playing every slasher flick nightmare ever conceived. Eva being chased by a hockey-mask-wearing Dimitri, who's holding a chain saw. A sobbing Eva chained to a wall, getting lashed. Eva naked and screaming on a bed while Dimitri—

"Fuck. Fuck!"

I blow out a breath and jerk upright, setting my feet on the floor. Doc looks at me.

"For what it's worth, I feel you. Love's the best thing in the world, but also the worst."

"Sounds like you're speaking from experience."

He gazes at me for a beat, then turns his head and stares at the ceiling. "I was married once."

The way he says it, the absolute rawness of his voice, makes me think his marriage didn't end in divorce. I say quietly, "Me too." When he glances at me again, I add, "Breast cancer."

He turns away, squeezing shut his eyes as if against a bad memory. After a moment he says, "Hit-and-run."

"Oh fuck. I'm sorry."

He swallows, then clears his throat. "Yeah. Date night. We got into a fight at dinner. Stupid shit, how I never helped around the house. Worked too much, whatever. She was right, but I was tired. Being an asshole. She got up from our table at the restaurant and ran out. I saw the whole thing, you know. We had a table by the window."

He stops abruptly. Then, more roughly: "Last thing I ever said to her was 'Stop being such a bitch.' Never got to apologize. She was gone by the time I got to her. Eyes wide open. Everything smashed. They never found the driver. Ten years ago, and I still dream about her all the time. Her face when I called her a bitch."

He stops again. This time he doesn't go on.

I sigh heavily, scrubbing my hands over my face. I know there's nothing I can say to help him, know that right now he's lost in his own personal hell of memory and regret.

If death teaches us anything, it's humility. And not to waste a single moment on the stupid shit because all of life is a ticking clock that will stop when you least expect it.

Over on the stainless-steel counter where he left it, Doc's cell phone rings.

I leap to my feet, heart pounding. Doc's on his feet, too, striding over to pick up the phone. Dragging the rolling metal IV stand I'm hooked up to along with me, I hurry over to him as he answers.

"Hello?" He listens for a moment, concentrating. "Hey, K." He glances at me. "Yeah. He's standing right here."

I shout, "What's he saying? Did he find Eva? What's going on?"

He crossly waves a hand for me to shut up. More listening, then he looks me up and down. "I gave him a pair of your trousers—no, jeans—and a sweatshirt—a plain black one, man—and a pair of your shoes. No, not the Ferragamos. Boots."

I say loudly, "They're too small."

Doc listens again, then makes a face. "No, I'm not gonna measure his feet!"

I roar, *"Does he have Eva?"*

Whatever Killian says makes Doc grimace. "Cheese and whiskers, you two are like a couple of chest-beating gorillas. Sorry, but I can't be the meat in your macho sandwich." He holds the cell out to me, shaking his head.

I snatch the cell and stick it against my ear. "Please fucking tell me you have her."

"I don't have her."

I drop the phone against my side, tilt my head back, and let rip a yell of frustration at the ceiling. Putting the phone back against my ear, I demand, "Tell me what's going on."

"What's going on is that I found one very dead man by the name of Vladimir Mikhailov at the bottom of a cellar on an abandoned estate in the countryside outside Warsaw—"

"You're in *Poland*? Gimme your exact location!"

His *tsk* of disappointment is infuriating. "The things you focus on. Now's not the time to get into your trust issues, mate."

I stay silent, seething, until he relents.

"All right, you bloody wanker. Get a pen."

"Doc. I need some paper and a pen." He produces it quickly, and I say to Killian, "Go."

I copy down the coordinates he gives me, then read them back to him to confirm. When I'm done, he says, "May I continue, or are you finished with the interrogation?"

I say through gritted teeth, "I haven't even *begun* with the interrogation."

"Anyway," he says, sighing, "our dead man kindly left behind his wallet and his cell phone. I'm sending you a pic of the ID now."

My heart leaps. "What kind of phone does he have?"

"Android."

"You can navigate to the Timeline page to see a map of everywhere he's been!"

Killian snorts. "Oh, really? Gee, I never would've thought of that. Thanks for the helpful tip."

God, this guy. I'd like to shave his eyebrows off while he's sleeping. "Tell me you have something good before I lose my mind."

In his pause, I can hear him smiling. "First things first. Tell me you're grateful I saved your life."

I drop the phone against my side again, taking deep breaths and counting to ten. When I put it back to my ear, I say as calmly as possible, "I'm grateful you saved my life."

He makes a disgruntled noise that indicates he's not entirely satisfied with my expression of gratitude.

I take more breaths, count a little higher. "Killian. I would like to share my sincere appreciation that you showed up when you did, and picked me up in the ambulance, and took me to your safe house, and called Doc to take care of all my holes. Thank you. Truly. From the bottom of my heart."

He's silent for a moment. In the background, I hear the distant boom of thunder.

"I can't tell if you're being sarcastic or not."

I almost throw the phone across the room, but instead scream several dozen obscenities as Doc watches from nearby, shaking his head. When I stop screaming, Killian is laughing.

"My God. That temper. You're a lit fuse, my friend."

At the top of my lungs, I thunder, *"Where's my woman?"*

He mutters, "Ugh. Me, Tarzan. You, Jane. Not an ounce of finesse." Then, in a normal voice: "I'll upload the data from the phone's SIM card and send it over. I'm sure you'll find it interesting. You and your crew can pore over it, make your plans. In the meantime, I've got other business to attend to. I'll check back with you soon."

Panic scuttles up my back, clamps icy claws around my throat, and squeezes. "Check back? What the hell are you talking about? Do you know where she is or not?"

He ignores my questions. "You've got the use of the safe house for as long as you want. Doc will give you anything you need. Cheers."

Then—unbelievably—he rings off.

I stand staring in shock at the phone in my hand until an electronic ding from across the warehouse distracts me. It's the computer bank. One of the many screens has lit up. Line after line of green text appears, scrolling quickly from top to bottom.

Doc says brightly, "Oh, look, code! I love it when he does that *Matrix* shit."

"Yeah," I say, scowling, already dialing Connor. "It's my favorite, too."

Half an hour later, Tabby has mapped every place our dead friend Vlad has visited within the past ninety days, dug up his school, criminal, driving, credit, and employment records, run background checks on his entire extended family and known associates, researched all the contacts in his phone, and cross-referenced the numbers and emails against whatever international hacker database she uses.

She's also downloaded his entire text message history, along with all his pictures.

Oh, the pictures. Vlad loved his penis more than air.

"I can honestly say, I've never seen a pair of testicles that big."

"They're like grapefruit! I wonder if he had to have his underwear custom made."

"Do you think it's a medical problem? It looks painful."

"I'm more interested in knowing why he has so many pictures of his junk. This collection is almost Smithsonian in scope. After scrolling through this gallery, I could pick this dude's frank and beans out of a police lineup."

Tabby, Connor, Doc, and I are on a conference call via a laptop Doc has provided. Doc sits at the bank of computers in a captain's chair while I pace behind him. He downloaded the data from Killian's uplink to the laptop and sent it to Tabby. The final thing we're waiting on is the identification of the owners, both business and residential, of all the addresses on Vlad's cell phone map.

In the meantime, voyeurism.

For them, anyway. I'm wearing a groove in the floor and fighting off the impending heart attack that wants to kill me.

"Okay, I've got the address report," says Tabby. The pictures of Vlad's dick vanish from the screen.

"Thank fuck," I say. "What've we got?"

She's silent awhile, examining the report, which is shown on our end as a small box on the upper-right side of the laptop's screen. The rest of the screen is an image of Tabby and Connor sitting beside each other at his big black desk in his office at Metrix.

She's wearing a pink T-shirt with the slogan STOP STARING AT MY TITS stretched across her tits. Her flaming red hair is in a ponytail. Her lips are painted scarlet. Her nails, black.

Connor looks his usual hulking, imposing self. One massive arm is slung around the back of his wife's chair. As she works, he toys with the end of her ponytail.

"We've got coffee shops. Restaurants. Dry cleaner's. Bank. The occasional strip club." She pauses, her fingers flying over the keyboard. "We've got his mother's and brother's homes, his friends' homes, uncle's, sister's, blah, blah, blah."

She pauses again for more typing, then makes a face. "We've got three different sperm banks, if you can believe it. Apparently those oversized testicles were earning him some pocket money."

Doc chuckles. "Way to make lemonade from your big lemons, dude."

Tabby glances at him, then at me, then shakes her head and goes back to typing.

"Here's the address match for the coordinates Killian gave you. It's a three-thousand-square-meter estate on a twenty-hectare parcel bought by Slavtek Corporation two months ago for eighteen million American dollars."

"Huge property," says Connor. "The house alone is thirty thousand square feet."

Without consulting a calculator to do the conversion from meters to feet, Tabby says, "Thirty-two thousand, two hundred ninety-one. Plus change."

Doc looks impressed, but Connor and I are already familiar with her formidable mind and take it in stride. I say, "A purchase by a corporation is a good way to hide the real owner."

Tabby smiles. "Let's see if our friends at Slavtek own anything else on this list." She turns to another computer on her desk and types in something. "Well, shit."

"What?"

"I've got *seventeen* properties here that are owned by this corporation."

"Anything in Saint Petersburg?"

Tabby knows what I'm thinking. "No. Dimitri's home in Russia was bought through his trust. I don't see any obvious tie-in between him and Slavtek, but I've got to research the corporation further."

I can't think of a reason why Dimitri would own so much property in Poland, but then again, who knows what that crazy fuck is up to. "Are all the properties Slavtek owns residential?"

Tabby clicks around for a minute. "Yes."

"Any of them bought within the last few months?"

"Yeah . . . all of them. And they're all enormous."

"So somebody's doing a property grab," says Doc, leaning back in his chair.

"Real estate's always a good investment," says Connor with a shrug.

I start to pace again, my mind a rat's nest of conspiracy theories, frustration, and anxiety. None of this seems to be getting us any closer to Eva.

So far, we haven't turned up any obvious connection between the dead guy Vladimir and Eva, except his body was in the last place we got a signal from Killian's business card GPS that she was carrying.

But that could mean anything. Maybe the guy picked up the card off the ground somewhere earlier, after Eva dropped it. Or maybe there really *wasn't* GPS in Killian's business card at all.

I stop pacing, frozen in horror.

Maybe this whole thing is a scam. A red herring, designed to make us look over *here* when Killian is doing something else he doesn't want us to notice over *there*.

I whirl on Doc, demanding, "Does Killian really have GPS in his business cards?"

"Does the pope wear funny hats?"

We stare at each other. I want to clobber him with my metal IV stand, until an even worse thought hits me.

Killian said he didn't *have* Eva, not that he didn't *find* her. And when I outright asked him if he knew where my woman was . . . he didn't answer.

"He operates on a need-to-know basis, and pretty much everything about him is do-not-need-to-know." I recall Doc's words about Killian, but now they have an entirely new meaning.

When I slam the IV stand on the ground in fury, Tabby and Connor both say, "What's wrong?"

"That bastard knows where she is!"

THIRTEEN

Eva

I pray.

On my knees, next to the bed, out of a lifetime of habit. *Dear Lord, please hear me. Dear Lord, please help me. Dear Lord, if you were standing in front of me now, I'd kick you right in your holy balls, you sanctimonious prick.*

Why give me something so beautiful only to snatch it away? What's the higher purpose in that? What could possibly be the point?

Yes, yes, I know. Suffering is the point. Testing my faith is the point. Seeing how high a mountain of shit I'm willing to climb in your name is the point.

Hallelujah.

Father, forgive me, but I just now realized you and Dimitri have a lot more in common than I thought.

I shift my weight from knee to knee, wincing at the stiffness in my legs. It's nothing compared to the stiffness in the rest of me, body and soul.

Naz is dead. The only man who ever made me feel safe and loved and *seen* is dead.

Yet here I am, surviving. Staring at this expensive white silk duvet cover, growing more and more atheist by the breath, wanting nothing more than to paint this whole room with Dimitri's blood.

I'm losing it.

Maybe I never had it to begin with.

Maybe I'm an artificial snowflake inside a plastic snow globe being shaken by a child in an alien galaxy in another dimension, millions of light-years away.

I'd cry if I weren't so stunned. I'm that deer straddling the double yellow lines in the middle of the highway, too shocked by the huge steel grille of the eighteen-wheeler bearing down on me to have the presence of mind to jump out of the way.

I don't bother turning when I hear a knock on the door. I simply wait for whatever comes.

"*Gospozha?*"

It's Stefan. Poor Stefan, who recently lost someone, too. I can't help but feel Vlad's death was my fault, though it was Dimitri who pulled the trigger. In a way, Dimitri was right: I should have known better. I knew the kind of devil I was dealing with.

So the body count to date is three. The Wolf—Dimitri's henchman sent to New York to kidnap me—the Wolf's companion, and Vlad. Four, actually, if I count Naz, who'd still be alive if he'd never met me.

And that angry dog at the apartment, too. So five.

No—that isn't it, either. How many of Dimitri's soldiers went to their final reward during that gun battle in the living room? Eight? Ten? Let's split the difference at nine. And let's not forget Raphael and the captain of the *Silver Shadow*, and the number is up to a whopping *sixteen* lives snuffed out, directly or indirectly, because of me.

Well. I'm really racking them up. One could say I've gone professional.

"*Gospozha?* May we come in?"

"Sure," I say dully to the duvet. "I'm just in here counting the corpses."

The door opens. After a moment, someone clears his throat.

"Madam. I'm here to put the cast on."

I look over my shoulder. There stand Stefan and the doctor, both looking at me with great concern. I wonder what my face is doing for these two men to look so alarmed. I rise unsteadily, then sit on the edge of the bed.

I should be lying down. The room has started, very gently, to spin.

The doctor walks closer, while Stefan retreats, closing and locking the doors. He knows better than to linger, due to the eyes in the walls.

The doctor stares at me in the white robe I put on when I returned to the suite from the fitting. He stares at my face and posture. "You look unwell."

Something inside my chest feels as if it's crumbling. My stomach is sour with bile. My pulse is erratic, and my hands and feet are ice cold. Looking at his shoes, I ask, "Can a person die of a broken heart?"

"Yes. There's actually a name for broken heart syndrome: takotsubo cardiomyopathy. It's caused by the heart's reaction to a surge of stress hormones brought on by divorce or death of a loved one."

"I'm guessing it probably wouldn't help if that person had heart problems to begin with."

After a moment of silence, the doctor drags a chair over from a table near the window. He sits down across from me and takes my hand.

"You're not going to die."

His gentle tone makes my eyes well with tears. I whisper, "What if I want to?"

"Then you think of all the reasons you need to live."

I glance up at him. He's gazing at me like a grandfather would, with affection and understanding, the wisdom of his years. He smiles. "I also recommend vodka. A few stiff drinks have helped me through many, many dark days."

"You're very kind. Thank you."

He drops his voice an octave. "Yes, I would think kindness is in short supply here."

I wonder how this gentle man came to work for Dimitri, but I don't ask. Spiders trap all sorts of different creatures in their webs.

I look down at his shoes again, and he pats my hand. Then he rises, sets the chair back in its place, and goes about the business of wrapping my broken arm in gauze and plaster, working silently until he's done.

"Keep it dry," he says when he's finished, packing up the bag he brought with him. "Your arm might itch, but don't stick anything inside the cast to try to scratch it. If you notice any bad odor or changes in the color of your fingers, call me right away. You'll be in the cast for at least a few weeks."

"I know," I tell him, because of course I've had casts before.

It's then that it hits me. Out of nowhere, stunning and unexpected, like a slap.

Rage.

Rage like a host of demons howling at the edge of an abyss, the stink of sulfur burning my eyes, an unholy fire scorching my veins, the sky raining brimstone that flays my skin and melts my bones to ashes. Bloody, bloodcurdling rage over all that I had, all that I've lost, and the child that I might be carrying who will never know her father.

Dimitri killed Naz.

Dimitri killed Naz.

I begin to shake so violently my teeth chatter.

The doctor doesn't notice. He's already turning and saying goodbye. He's crossing to the door and knocking, because he knows it's locked. He's in my cage.

I'm in a cage.

Dimitri killed Naz.

What the hell am I doing sitting here like nothing happened?

The door opens. The doctor passes through. I see Stefan's face, those sharp cat eyes missing nothing, taking in my incandescent fury with unblinking steadiness, as if he was waiting for it. As if he knew it would be coming.

I jolt to my feet, fly across the room, and throw the door wide open, slamming it against the wall. The doctor turns, startled. Stefan merely waits.

Like a banshee, I scream, *"Take me to that son of a bitch right now!"*

On Stefan's face, the faintest hint of a smile.

⁂

Dimitri's study is on the opposite end of the manor, past a dizzying array of rooms I pay no notice to. I don't pay any notice, either, to the startled looks of the staff who recoil, as if from a plague, as I storm by, or to the whispers that rise in my wake. I might look like a Valkyrie on bad acid with my wild, vengeful eyes and bared teeth, but so be it. I don't care how I look.

I've got blood to spill.

Stefan raps his knuckles on the big wooden doors we stop in front of, holding up a hand to tell me to wait. Panting and vibrating with anger, almost frothing at the mouth like something rabid, it's all I can do not to bite his fingers off.

When we hear the "Come" from within, I push past Stefan and explode into the room like a grenade.

Sitting behind a wide oak desk across the room, Dimitri looks me over dispassionately, with nothing like fear. Or even surprise. It's like he knew I was coming.

He swirls the whiskey in the cut crystal glass in his hand. "This should be interesting. Have you found a gun?"

He's stripped to the waist. His strong, lean chest glistens with a sheen of sweat. The muscles of his stomach are clenched, each individual one articulated, as if they're under strain.

Kneeling on the floor beside his chair is his physician who looks like an accountant. He's surprised by my sudden entrance, blinking like an owl. He was in the midst of cleaning the bullet hole in Dimitri's abdomen.

The hole that is as red and angry as my face and surrounded by a mottled landscape of purple and waxy white flesh marbled with a network of veins that resemble blue cheese.

To one side of Dimitri's desk is a bank of security cameras showing hallways and bedrooms, living areas and driveways, the kitchen and dining room and everything else. I see a maid enter my room and start to vacuum, and my fury that was a wretched, broken thing gathers itself into a diamond-hard shaft of vengeance, edges glinting like sunlight off a sword.

I grind out words through a clenched jaw. "No. But this will work."

I run to the unlit fireplace, grab the iron poker from the stand on the hearth, and whirl around, brandishing it.

"Now, now, Evalina. Don't be melodramatic."

That dripping condescension. He's not worried, but he will be. "I haven't even *started* the melodrama yet. Brace yourself."

I smash the glass on the front of a nearby bookcase with a single stroke. My left arm is useless, but my right is more than happy to make up for the deficiency. After the bookcase, I smash two empty porcelain vases on the fireplace mantel along with a glass bust of Stalin that explodes into a million glinting shards. Then I whirl around again, breathing heavily, my palms slick with sweat.

Dimitri regards me with amusement. Like I'm an adorable kitten, scratching the furniture, climbing up the curtains with a bushy tail.

"I must admit, this is unexpected. I suppose you picked up all these violent tendencies from your time with the American."

He smiles, knowing the mention of Naz will infuriate me even more, which it does.

Dimitri's always armed, even without a weapon.

I advance, slowly, steadily, the poker clenched in my shaking fist. "I'm going to kill you."

He sighs, finishing off the whiskey with a flourish and setting down the glass. "Dearest," he says mockingly, "I'm enjoying this game, but as you can see, at the moment I'm otherwise occupied. So we'll have to reschedule."

He pulls a pistol from the top drawer of his desk.

I freeze.

He sets the pistol down on the blotter in front of him, turns it so the barrel is facing me, then laces his hands over his bare stomach, his movements unhurried. "Unless you're in a gambling mood. You're, what, four meters away? Do you think you could run over here and smash in my skull with that poker before I could pick up the gun and shoot you in the chest?"

The *hubris* of this man. His arrogance is matched only by his depravity.

I glance at the gun, then back at him, calculating the distance between us.

And making him laugh.

"Look at you, little cobra, coiling up to strike." He rubs a finger over his full bottom lip, blue eyes alight with anticipation, then leans over his desk. His voice grows husky. "Come on, then, love. Come and get me."

The doctor rises and scuttles past me sideways like a crab, hurrying to retreat to the safety of the doorway, where Stefan still stands.

Dimitri and I stare at each other.

He has one of those endless unblinking gazes you could lose your soul in, a stare so chilling it sinks icy fingers right down to your bones. The urge to hurt him—to *kill* him—is a jungle drumbeat inside me, loud and ugly, hot and vicious. My teeth grind against each other. A spasm of hatred contracts my stomach to a fist.

I once thought love was a foolish fancy. Like self-pity, something I couldn't afford. But then I met a man who taught me that love isn't foolish, it's necessary. Elemental. The one thing without which we cannot truly live.

My movement is expulsive. The rocket fuel of fury makes wings of my feet. I'm on Dimitri before he understands what happened, before he believes his own eyes that I could have possibly gotten to him so fast.

But probably not before he feels the hard bite of iron against his face.

My swing is awkward but true. The poker slams into his jaw with a satisfying *crack*. His head snaps to the side. He roars in outrage and pain. Blood sprays a hot, wet stripe across my chest.

A small white object flies past: a tooth.

He topples out of the chair and falls to the floor on his hands and knees, shaking his head like a dog to clear it. Seeing him like that—wounded, bleeding, humiliated—gives me a surge of power as if I've stuck my finger into an electrical socket.

Standing at the side of his desk, I shout down at him, "By the way, *dearest*, there's something I've been meaning to say. *Fuck you!*"

I take another wild swing, but he's recovered from the shock of my surprise attack. He's already rising, staggering to his feet. He manages to avoid another hit with a lucky jerk to one side just as the poker whizzes past his nose. Then he launches himself at me, tackling me in a bear hug and slamming me facedown onto his desk.

The poker falls from my hand. The wind is knocked out of me, and I briefly see stars. My arm in its cast burns in agony.

He's monstrously heavy on top of me, his arms binding mine, his breath hot in my ear. He croons, "No, my love. Fuck *you*."

He fumbles at his waist with one hand, unbuckling his belt.

I scream in frustration, kicking my legs, but he's too strong to budge. The pistol was knocked off the desk onto the carpet, within arm's reach if I could stretch, but my only working arm is pinned underneath me. I try frantically to wriggle it free, but Dimitri forces his forearm down against my neck, his hand gripping my shoulder in an iron vise, holding it in place.

I send a desperate glance to the doorway, but Stefan and the doctor are gone.

Dimitri wedges a leg between mine. The sound of his belt flying through belt hooks seems unnaturally loud, a slithery *zizz* that makes me scream again, this time in terror.

His hand fumbles under my robe, yanking it up to my waist, then clamping down on my hip. His nails bite into my bare skin.

When he pulls his zipper down, he laughs. It's a crazy sound, obscene, like laughter at a funeral.

I struggle underneath him, every muscle straining, my breath coming in panicked gasps. I feel something sharp against my belly, a cold edge digging into my flesh, but I'm fighting like an animal to get free from the snarling weight of Dimitri, who's holding my hips down and angling himself to gain entrance. He pants with lust as I buck and flail.

"Come now, Eva," he says in a rasp of a voice, thrilled by my fear and desperate cries. "Let me give you what you need."

That thing under my belly. That sharp, flattened thing—what is it?

I relax for a heartbeat, my pulse a thrum like wingbeats in my ears, my mind an echo chamber of *No No No* repeating in an unceasing silent scream.

Dimitri makes a grunt of victory at what he mistakes as surrender. He removes his forearm from my neck to get a better grip on things down below.

Without his weight bearing down on me, I can move my hand. My fingers close around the flat object smashed between the desk and my womb. As soon as I feel the cool touch of metal against my fingertips, I know what it is.

And I know what to do with it.

My body is strong, honed by years of daily dance practice, hours and hours spent at the barre, conditioning and toning my muscles, training them to not only endure pain but to accept it and work past it, to allow it a place at the table. Not exactly a friend but more a respected adversary.

But my *flexibility*. Now that's where I really shine.

In one fluid, whip-crack twist, I snap my upper body around and embed the letter opener into the soft spot under Dimitri's chin.

FOURTEEN

NAZ

I pace back and forth like a caged lion, so enraged that for several moments I can't speak.

Tabby and Connor watch me from the laptop screen as Doc slowly rolls away in his captain's chair to a safer distance.

When I hurled the IV stand to the ground, the bag of antibiotics popped off the hook. It drags behind me now on its plastic tube like a severed limb, still hanging on by a few strings of meat. I stop, rip the needle out of the back of my hand, and throw that down, too, before starting to stalk back and forth again.

Limp back and forth, technically. On top of the slight hitch in my stride I already had from an old injury, my stitched-up calf is screaming.

So are my lungs. Muscles. Gut.

Heart.

"I don't even know if those coordinates Killian gave me are where he actually went," I say, almost spitting with fury. "I have no proof of anything!"

"We do have the dead guy, though," says Doc, overly bright. When I cut him a lethal glare, he holds up his hands in a placating gesture. "Just saying."

"*Do* we have a dead guy?" I insist. I can feel all the veins sticking out in my neck. "Who knows who this fucking Vladimir what's-his-name really is? We don't have anything that concretely ties him to Dimitri *or* Eva! Maybe he's one of Killian's superspy buddies!"

"I don't think Killian has 'buddies.' He's more the lone-wolf type."

"How do I know that? I don't know *anything* about him! I don't know if Killian is his real name, I don't know who he works for, I don't know where he went or how he got there, or even, especially, *what his plans are for my woman!*"

Doc doesn't seem impressed by my rant. He kicks one sneakered foot up over his opposite thigh, shrugging. "I mean, yeah, you have to accept a certain amount of ambiguity when you're dealing with him, but . . ." He hesitates for a moment, as if considering if it's wise to go on. "He did sorta save your life."

The pressure behind my eyeballs is dangerously high. I wouldn't be at all surprised if they popped out of my head and splattered against the wall.

Before I can get into all the particulars about how exactly Killian did *not* save my life, Tabby says urgently, "I've got something."

Feeling like I could be having a stroke, I lurch over to the laptop and slap my palms on the desk. "What is it?"

"This guy, this friend of Vlad's. Stefan."

A picture pops up in the small box on the right-hand side of the screen. Taken from straight on as the subject is walking toward the camera, it shows a man in his early thirties, built, dark haired, with a short dark beard and penetrating green eyes. He's dressed in black slacks and a white button-down dress shirt rolled up his corded forearms, both of which look like they could be cutting off circulation they're so tight. Obviously, he's proud of his physique.

Even more obviously, he's dangerous. His whole vibe screams "badass."

"Who is he?"

"Former commander in the Russian Armed Forces. Post-military career consists mainly of personal security for sketchy dudes. Oligarchs, Mafia heads, the occasional fascist. But a few months ago, he started a new gig. He brought his friend Vlad with him."

Her smile tells me everything I need to know about who Stefan's new employer is.

"Dimitri."

"Yep."

My stroke is now fighting for dominance with the surge of endorphins flooding my bloodstream with euphoria.

A lead. At last.

"How do we know?"

She says archly, "Oh, you want all the technical particulars?"

"I promise I'm not second-guessing you," I say placatingly, knowing how much she hates that. "I'm just thirsty for anything solid I can get right now."

She quirks her lips. "Suit yourself."

She presses a key on her keyboard, and my screen floods with data. Window after window pops up. I see screenshots of text messages with highlighted names. I see maps with pinned addresses. I see lists of phone numbers. I see bank statements. I see a bunch of other reports that I can't understand, because everything is in Russian.

"Good to go on my end," I say brightly, knowing I'm outwitted but loath to admit it. "What's next?"

"Of the seventeen properties the Slavtek Corporation owns, Vlad and Stefan exchanged texts at or about twelve of them. And one of them is from the address Killian gave you, which also happens to be where Vlad's last text originated."

Doc sends me a dour granny-face look, like *I told you.*

"Show me the other addresses."

A map takes over the screen. On it are eleven pinned locations, approximately thirty kilometers apart, all in countryside locations outside Warsaw. Another pin shows the coordinates Killian gave me over the phone.

"Okay, you secretive prick," I mutter, staring hard at the map. "Which one of those other addresses did you run off to?"

Doc is incredulous. "Don't tell me you're going *after* him."

I straighten and look at him. "No, I'm not going after him. I'm going after Eva. And I'm doing it *now.*"

"You're practically dead!"

"Thanks for that, but I'm not even a little bit dead."

"You're full of holes! You could get sepsis!"

"Yeah, well, I could also drop at any time from a heart attack. I'll take my chances."

Doc stands, turning to beseech Tabby and Connor on the laptop. "This is a terrible plan. I mean, *awful.* Not only is your boy in no shape to go gallivanting around the globe—"

Connor snorts. "Gallivanting?"

"—but there's no evidence Eva is at any of those locations!"

I say, "My gut tells me she is."

He turns and stares at me, then at my stomach. "Your *gut?* You mean your gut that recently suffered a penetrating trauma? *That* gut? The gut that could be harboring bacteria that entered the wound via the bullet and could be, as we speak, incubating disaster? The gut that hasn't eaten anything in, oh, I don't know, a *really* long time?"

Feeling much better now that I have a clear plan of attack and I'm not leaving Eva's fate up to my semi-archenemy, Killian, I say, "You've been dosing me with meds for the past day, remember? So I'm not incubating anything. And I'll have a breakfast bar before I leave."

Doc's voice climbs an octave. *"A breakfast bar?"*

I turn to the screen and look at Tabby and Connor. "Will someone please tell my grandma that I'm a grown man?"

He throws his hands in the air. "Oh, that's right. I forgot I was dealing with the idiot who refused anesthetic before a surgical procedure."

"I've been shot before, Doc."

He stares balefully at me. "If you tell me you stitched yourself up like Stallone did in the jungle in *First Blood*, we can't be friends anymore."

I just stand there and look at him, because I'm not the type to brag.

He shakes his head and turns away, muttering, "I give up."

I turn my attention back to Tabby and Connor. "See if you can get satellite imagery on all those locations. I'm going in."

Tabby says, "Let's hook you up with Günter and his boys. They can scout some of them for you—"

"Negative," I say forcefully. "I can't trust that crew not to stop for pizza or sightseeing. Plus they're about as stealthy as a herd of stampeding elephants. If anyone's watching, they'll see the Germans coming from miles away. I have to do this solo so it doesn't go sideways. Let's talk logistics. Then I'm gonna need exfil to Poland as soon as you can arrange it.

"And guns. A *lot* of guns."

FIFTEEN

EVA

Dimitri's eyes go wide. Warmth spurts over my hand and down my arm, and it's his blood.

He staggers back, clutching his throat, making awful gurgling noises. His face is disfigured by astonishment.

As soon as he's off me, I scramble away, but clumsily, so I fall over the desk and hit the floor. I grab the pistol, stand, and whirl around.

Incredibly, Dimitri is still standing, too.

Swaying a little, his face white and his lips peeled back over his teeth, he glares at me with those icy blue eyes bulging in outrage. He curls his fingers around the letter opener, then slowly pulls it from his flesh. He flings it aside and clasps his hand over the spurting wound.

Shining with blood, his bare chest heaves, but he doesn't fall.

He doesn't fall.

My heart thundering, I raise the pistol and take aim at the center of his chest. My finger curls around the trigger—

"Stop!"

I look over my shoulder just in time to see Dimitri's guards swarm into the room. The one who shouted stands in front, his rifle already trained on me. The others quickly follow suit.

My brain explodes with panic. If I shoot Dimitri, I'll be dead in seconds. If I don't shoot him . . .

I'll only wish I were.

The baby, Eva! Think of the baby! What if you're pregnant? You can't die!

There's a moment of crackling silence, electric, before Dimitri lunges at me and yanks the gun from my grip. He backhands me so hard it knocks me off my feet.

I hit the floor with my broken arm beneath me, all my weight atop. I cry out, arching in agony, but can't roll away because Dimitri smashes his foot down on the inside of my thigh, brutally hard. I scream and struggle, until I see him raise the pistol and point it at my stomach.

Purely on instinct, I cover my belly with my good arm and curl around it, drawing up to protect it and screaming, *"No!"*

Dimitri's foot grinds down on my leg. He coughs, a wet, ugly sound. A fine spray of blood splatters my face. When I glance up at him, he's holding the gun in one hand and pressing the other against his throat.

He should be bleeding more! He shouldn't be standing! How is he still standing?

The chaos of my thoughts is interrupted when Dimitri narrows his eyes—

And looks at my belly.

I realize my mistake, but too late. He's already removing his foot from my leg and stepping back to take aim at the place I moved so quickly to protect moments ago.

I thrust up a hand and scream again. *"No!"*

Then I watch as the light of understanding dawns in the monster's eyes.

He blinks, the rage clearing into something far more terrifying. He looks from my stomach to my face and back again, then starts to laugh. A choking, phlegmy laugh that's something right out of a nightmare. It's not really laughter at all, but horrible gurgles of glee between wet rasps of breath. His teeth are bared, and they're bloody.

He knows.

One of the guards shouts out the doorway for the doctor. The rest of them slowly advance until they've surrounded me. Still aiming the pistol at my stomach, Dimitri drops heavily into an armchair across from me, sweating and disheveled, his eyes bright with victory.

Between gritted teeth, in a hideous swamp croak of a voice thick with blood, he manages to speak.

"You're pregnant."

I huddle on the floor in panic, shaking, terrified, my heart beating out of my chest.

When I don't answer, he nods to himself, then starts his awful boggy laugh again, his shoulders shaking with mirth until he's overcome by coughing. He turns his head and spits out a mouthful of blood onto the carpet.

Dimitri's doctor hurries into the room. Shoving aside the guards, he approaches Dimitri with exclamations of shock, coaxing him to sit back so he can inspect the wound.

No one makes a sound as the doctor examines Dimitri. Every weapon in the room is pointed at me. I cower, shivering with fear, as Dimitri is made to open his mouth. The doctor gently pokes around, lifting Dimitri's tongue, palpating his neck, clucking with consternation.

All the while, Dimitri stares at me, his blue eyes glittering.

This is the closest I've ever seen him to true happiness. I've given him a gift of incalculable scope, a gift that is the key to my total submission, my complete domination, my utter acquiescence of will.

Naz's baby is the best leverage Dimitri could ever gain over me. By far the most powerful leverage of all.

The doctor says, "Judging by the pattern of bleeding, it appears the carotid artery and jugular vein are intact, but the tongue and the underlying muscles have been pierced. The soft palate is untouched. There could be some damage to the vagus nerve—"

Dimitri impatiently jerks his hand for the doctor to summarize.

"It's not a lethal wound. You'll have swelling and possibly infected salivary glands. And of course tremendous pain—"

Dimitri shoves him away, pointing at me. Through a clenched jaw, he rasps, "Examine her for pregnancy."

The doctor turns to me with lifted brows.

I try to stall by sputtering, "I-I'm not pregnant."

He looks me over, then turns back to Dimitri. "She certainly doesn't appear to be. A urine test will confirm it."

"Do it."

He nods. "I'll clean the wound first—"

"*Now.*"

The doctor knows better than to argue. He simply says, "I'll be back within the hour. Keep pressure on it until the bleeding stops."

He scurries off to get the pregnancy test that will seal my fate.

I don't want to think of what will happen if I'm *not* pregnant. There are no happy endings to this story either way.

Dimitri snaps his fingers, points at me, then jerks his thumb toward the door. The guards understand they're to take me to my suite.

They drag me from the room on my useless feet. I tell myself over and over not to cry, that it will be all right, somehow there will be a miracle, something will happen to save me.

But even as I silently repeat the words, I don't believe them. Naz is gone. My white knight can't save anyone anymore. If any saving is going to happen, I'll have to do it myself.

God help me.

I'm shoved through the doors of the suite by the guard with the broken nose who took such pleasure in seeing me naked during the fitting. He slams and bolts the doors behind me, then he leaves me alone to nurse my ballooning hysteria.

Stefan wasn't with him. He wasn't one of the guards who had me surrounded in Dimitri's study, either. Did he call Killian? Is he even still at the house? What is he doing with the information I gave him? Is there a chance he can intervene in any way?

What am I going to do?

My helplessness and panic are unbearable.

To manage them, I start to break things.

I hurl a marble vase against the window to see if Dimitri told me the truth about the glass being unbreakable. He did. The only thing I succeed in doing is shattering the vase into a chunky spray of white marble that scatters on the carpet, but the window is unscathed.

Next, I throw a table lamp against the wall. It doesn't produce much of a satisfying smash. The lampshade pops off, and the clear acrylic base cracks, but it falls to the floor mostly intact. Then I work my way methodically around the room, tearing paintings off walls, toppling pedestals with nude statues, kicking over tables and chairs. Sweating and gasping for air, I charge into the closet and start tearing clothes from their padded silk hangers, throwing them into a pile in the middle of the floor.

I know it's useless. A worthless waste of energy better spent planning how to handle this unthinkable situation. But if I don't do something productive with all my impotent fear and rage, I'm liable to hurt myself . . .

A terrible thought steals through my head, jerking me upright and leaving me shaking. I walk slowly into the bathroom and stare at the amber bottle of painkillers on the counter by the sink.

If I'm not pregnant, if it comes to that . . .

No. Suicide is a sin. I'll be damned.

Ha! You think you're not damned already? What's your body count at now?

I don't understand why my inner voice has to be such a bitch.

Turning my back on the bathroom, I stagger back into the closet and sink down into the middle of the pile of couture.

I'm still sitting there, shaking, when the doctor returns.

It's a pharmacy test he brings with him, one of those pee-on-a-stick kits you can find at drugstores. I used to see them at my neighborhood *farmacia* in Cozumel and wonder if I'd ever be lucky enough to find myself in need of one.

I'm in need of one now, but *lucky* is the last word I'd use to describe this situation.

He opens the box, unwraps the stick from its plastic wrapper, and stands in the bathroom waiting for me.

When I take it from his fingers, he says without apology, "I have to watch. You understand."

I understand nothing except I'm doomed no matter what the outcome. When I sit on the toilet and hold the uncapped stick under my stream of urine, I'm as cold as Siberian tundra.

"Give it to me when you've finished," instructs the doctor. I hold it out to him, and he takes the stick with a gloved hand. He doesn't bother turning away when I wipe and flush.

Then he stands there staring at the stick as I sit on the toilet cover, wishing I could die.

For minutes, silence. Then the doctor looks at me.

"Congratulations."

He turns and leaves before he sees me slip to my knees on the floor.

Dimitri finds me like that, kneeling on the bathroom floor in front of the toilet, in a shock so deep it's bottomless. He's still shirtless, his neck and chest still painted with his own blood, though it's dried to grue-some flaking streaks. His stomach has a fresh bandage, and now there's a bandage on his throat, too.

In his hand he holds a corded leather whip.

He gazes down at me from the doorway, blond and beautiful, his smile like a sunrise, his eyes killer blue.

"Stand up."

The softness of his tone is sickening. We both know he doesn't have to ever raise his voice to me again.

I rise unsteadily and face him, not bothering to try to hide my disgust.

When he moves toward me, I hold still, and I keep still when he takes my face in his hands. Looking deeply into my eyes, he speaks in the tender tone of a lover. It's perverse.

"If you disobey or disrespect me again, even once, even slightly, I'll cut that baby out of you with a kitchen knife. Do you understand?"

How am I standing? The world has fallen out from under my feet. I say shakily, "Yes."

"Good. Take off the robe."

Oh God. Oh God not this. Don't think. Don't think just do it just do it just hurry up. My fumbling fingers find the way of it through my horror and their shaking, and the robe puddles around my ankles on the floor.

Without speaking another word, Dimitri grabs me by the scruff of the neck and forces me to bend over the counter, shoving my face against the marble. When he kicks my legs apart, I squeeze my eyes shut and bite back a sob.

It isn't penetration he has in mind, however. It's punishment.

And this whipping makes the one in the cellar look like child's play.

The blows rain down on my bare skin with unleashed savagery, each accompanied by a snarl. I jump and scream with every bite of the whip. My screams grow louder as my flesh burns, the pain so huge it has its own atmosphere, its own temperature, its own weight. I can do nothing but submit and endure, though it's beyond enduring, a white-hot center of misery that extinguishes everything else. After one particularly brutal volley of slashes to my upper thighs, I'm sure I'll pass out from the agony.

But then it's over.

My tormentor staggers back, panting from exertion.

I slide off the counter and collapse against the cold marble, its snowy-white surface freckled red with my blood.

"The ceremony is at sunset tomorrow," he says, gasping for breath. "Make sure you're rested. You'll have a long wedding night ahead."

When I raise my head and gaze at him through watering eyes, his expression is exultant. He spins around and stalks off, his shoulders gleaming with sweat, his gait unsteady, the whip gripped so tightly in his hand his knuckles are white.

I'm still lying on the floor, shaking convulsively, when the mute maid finds me. She pulls a towel off the towel rack and covers me with it, then kneels down beside me and takes my head into her lap. When I meet her gaze, her eyes well with pity.

I want to tell her not to feel sorry for me yet because things are going to get far worse, but instead I merely close my eyes and whimper, and let the marble have my blood.

⁓

The maid does her best to clean my skin with cool cloths and make me comfortable. Her hands are gentle, but she has to keep stopping when my moans become too pitiful to ignore. When she tries to give me something for the pain, I refuse.

I can't take anything until I ask the doctor how it will affect the baby.

The baby. Naz's baby. *Our* baby. My joy that a part of him will live on is almost obliterated by the intimate knowledge of the hell our child will be born into.

Her mother will be a slave, and she'll be a captive.

Or worse.

My mind skitters away from what *worse* might entail, but keeps coming back to it. Picking at it, the way you might pick at a scab.

How will Dimitri treat a child? Especially a child not his own?

Especially a *girl* child? Dear God, what if the baby is a girl?

I shudder to think of it, but I can't risk another escape attempt, not if my child's life is the price of failure. And another try at ending Dimitri will be impossible. He'll be wary of me now that he's seen how hard I can scratch. He'll never let his guard down or make the mistake of underestimating me again.

Allowing the baby to be born into this nightmare is something I have to prevent, but I don't have any hope of succeeding. The total *absence* of hope is a hollow ache inside me. Hope extinguished, ripped inside out. A fairy tale turned into a horror story because the evil beast that should have been vanquished killed the prince, captured the princess, and burned the castle down.

The maid helps me to the bed. I collapse onto it in a daze, barely noticing when she leaves. I lie on my belly with my face buried in the pillows and my flayed skin throbbing until she returns with ice and salve. When she presses the ice to my skin, I hiss and jerk but force myself to remain still, clenching the blankets in my fist.

By the time she's finished icing my back, bottom, and legs, I can no longer fight off the blackness wrapping its arms around me. I tumble into darkness with Naz's name a murmured plea on my lips.

Tomorrow is my wedding day.

And the funeral of every dream I dared to dream.

SIXTEEN

Eva

Morning comes. With it comes sickness that has me hobbling into the bathroom to retch over the toilet. And retch.

And retch.

It's more than morning sickness. It's heartsickness, too. *Soul* sickness. I'm ill straight down to the marrow of my bones.

The day dawned with the ominous sign of thunderstorms. Ominous but appropriate. I stand at the windows and stare up at the glowering sky. The clouds are lead gray and oppressive, hovering low to the ground and spitting rain. Intermittent bursts of jagged white lightning claw through. The bass boom of thunder rattles the windows. The smell of rain and ozone perfumes the air.

There's something else in the air, too, but I can't put my finger on what it is. Something charged. Watchful. I feel it underlying my dread, feel it all around me, something dark, tense, and filled with anticipation, like a held breath.

It's there in Stefan's darting eyes when he lets in the maid to attend to me. It's in the distracted way she moves, in the slight shaking of her hands when she helps me bathe and dress. It's in the pinched mouth and drawn brows of the stout gray-haired woman who brings me my breakfast on a silver platter, rolled in on a cart laid with white linen and a long-stemmed white rose. She barely even glances at the wreckage I made of the room.

When I tell her thank you, she answers quietly in German without looking up. "You're welcome, madam."

I recognize her voice. It's Astrid, the voice on the phone. The friendly kitchen maid who isn't so friendly today.

Her manner warns me off from small talk. Whatever has the staff spooked, it piques my curiosity, but I've got so many other disasters to think on, I let it pass.

A few hours after my untouched breakfast is removed, the vans begin to arrive.

I glimpse them from afar, winding up the main driveway like a funeral procession, headlights on as they creep along at half speed. My window is a poor vantage point, only allowing me to see a sliver of the sweeping front lawns and paved drive from my room, but as the vans turn around a curve and go out of sight, I glimpse the business logos on their sides.

The words are all in Polish, unrecognizable.

Kwiaty. Ciasto. Żywnościowy.

Even unrecognizable, they strike me cold with fear.

Hours pass. No one comes. The storm grows worse, battering the windows with rain, bending the trees with howling winds. The day wanes, growing darker. I have the sense of being lost in time, of being forgotten, stranded in my wrecked prison in some abandoned corner of the world.

Then I'm found again.

I leap at the sound of knuckles rapping on the door. I'd been pacing in front of the windows, lost in my thoughts, but now I whirl around, heart thumping. "Yes?"

Stefan unlocks the doors and swings them open. Two women I've never seen before enter. They're young, slim, dressed in black, wearing too much makeup and heavy perfume. They both carry identical white plastic tackle boxes, the kind fishermen use to store lures.

Stefan carries a long white garment bag, a smaller glossy blue bag with silk ribbon handles, and a rectangular black velvet box the size of a hardback novel. He gazes at me steadily for a moment, then drapes the bag over the back of the nearest chair, sets the box and blue bag on a side table, and leaves without looking back.

I know I didn't imagine the tense line of his shoulders, the way his eyes clung to mine. My rising panic isn't a figment of my imagination, either.

I know exactly what's in that bulky white garment bag. Custom measured to fit with yards of silk, lace, and humiliation.

The girls begin to chatter at me. In Polish.

"I don't understand," I say, shaking my head.

They look at each other, then coerce me to sit on the edge of the bed with pantomime and gentle pushes. The one with black hair in a low chignon opens her tackle box, exposing its innards, a confusion of colorful tubes, bottles, brushes, and powders. The other one begins to brush my hair.

I sit—bottom throbbing—and breathe shallowly as the girls transform me.

When they're done, the one with the chignon holds a hand mirror up to my face. I almost laugh, but dismay smothers it. I'm so rouged and powdered I hardly recognize myself, with an exaggerated cat's-eye liner, theatrical blush, and contouring in the hollows of my cheeks. My red lips are a bloodlike slash across my face, lurid against my pale skin. I look like a cliché of a nineteenth-century streetwalker in the back alleys of Montmartre, all paint and desperation.

They did a passable job covering up the bruising around the stitches under my eye, but nothing can be done about the swelling or the Frankenstein sutures of black thread, puckered and uneven. It was a careless job and will leave an ugly scar.

Another one to add to my growing collection.

They leave, and Stefan lets the maid in to assist me with my dress. This time he doesn't look at me.

When the maid unzips the garment bag, it erupts in a froth of white, spilling finery from its guts. Burning with hatred and loathing, I stare at the dress and matching veil and forcibly will myself not to rip them both to shreds with my teeth.

The maid stands there a moment with a pitying look, wringing her hands.

"It's okay," I tell her, the hugest lie I've ever told. "Let's just get this over with."

I realize I said the exact same thing to Vlad. It will probably become my new motto: Let's just get this over with. Let's do this horrible thing so I can get on with all the rest of the horrible things lined up for me next.

With thunder clapping against the leaden bowl of the sky, I don my wedding gown. Lightning flashes. Rain streams down the windows like tears. Then it's done, and I'm standing in front of the bathroom mirror staring at my reflection in a combination of revulsion and horror so profound that for several long minutes, I'm unable to speak.

It's profane that I'm marrying Dimitri and not Naz.

It's so wrong there isn't a word for it.

The maid brings in the blue bag that Stefan left, along with the black velvet box. The bag produces a pair of elegant strappy sandals, high heeled, beaded with crystals. How Dimitri expects me to walk in them I don't know, considering the sorry state of my legs. I doubt I'll be able to keep my balance.

The black velvet box opens to reveal a spectacular diamond necklace and matching earrings. The gems sparkle with icy brilliance as the maid fastens the necklace around my neck. I look at their flashing beauty, feeling nothing at all.

So this is what hell is. Thunder and lightning and the sky raining tears, silk and diamonds and the devil who awaits to lead you into desolation.

"I thought it would be hotter," I muse, absently touching the large stone nestled in the hollow of my throat.

The maid looks at me strangely. I don't bother to explain.

Another maid enters and hands me a bouquet of white roses.

Then it's time to begin.

⌘

Stefan is the one who leads me through the cool, silent corridors of the manor, walking in front of me like an usher. Or, more accurately, a prison guard. He's changed into a suit and tie, both somber black, funeral attire, which strikes me as darkly hilarious.

I trail behind him, shattered with grief, in a kind of muted hysteria that threatens to break free when I take too deep a breath.

Screams are trapped in my throat. The bouquet trembles in my hands. With every step, I fray a little more around the edges.

Because my back is as raw as ground meat, the maid used an entire roll of gauze on me so I didn't bleed through the silk, though now I think it would have been better if I had. More honest, anyway. Let everyone see exactly what Dimitri has made me. The open wound I am. The silly little bird who dared to fly free of her cage and wound up broken instead.

"You're not broken. You're just bent."

Tabby said that to me a lifetime ago, and I never forgot it. I think she'd change her mind if she saw me now.

We round a corner, and the drawing room yawns open before us. The room is full to bursting with vases of fresh white Casablanca lilies, so full I almost swoon from their overpowering sickly-sweet scent. If there were anything in my stomach, it would make a reappearance and make a mess of the polished wood floor.

I falter when I see Dimitri near the fireplace speaking to a priest.

Dimitri is in all black, too, like Stefan, but unlike Stefan he's leaning heavily on a cane. The sight of that cane gives my soul whiplash. He must be seriously injured to allow himself to appear in front of others under anything but perfect control.

He must be seriously injured.

I recall the way his stomach looked yesterday when the doctor was cleaning it, that disgusting, waxy blue cheese mottling around the wound, and experience a moment of elation so sharp and hot a gasp of joy slips past my lips.

His bullet wound is infected. Maybe the wound on his neck is, too. If he's not taking the right antibiotics, or enough of them . . . he could die.

And Dimitri's is exactly the kind of arrogance that would insist he didn't need antibiotics in the first place. After all, gods can heal their own wounds.

At the sound of my gasp, he turns, which is when my soul almost jumps from my body in fright.

The left side of his face where I hit him with the poker is swollen with a garish purple-blue contusion. Above the stiff collar of his dress shirt, his throat is also swollen, but grotesquely, as if from a tumor. The bandage that covers the place I stabbed him is a small square of antiseptic white against what otherwise looks like a very bad problem.

A very bad problem indeed.

Into the sudden silence, my laugh seems too loud.

"Glad to see you in such high spirits," says Dimitri, his look lethal, his jaw clenched. "Get your ass over here."

He speaks with difficulty, the words thick. His tongue must be swollen, too. I hope his brain swells up and leaks out his ear canals.

I walk slowly to where he stands, my gaze demurely lowered. The laugh was a mistake, but one that couldn't be helped. I'll have to be more careful now. Even weakened, apex predators are deadly.

When I'm close enough, he seizes my arm and drags me against his body, sniffing my throat like a wolf. "How do you like your wedding gift?" He jerks his chin at the diamonds around my neck.

"Very beautiful," I say, my gaze still downcast. Then, as if it wasn't obvious, as if I myself weren't the cause of his punctures and bruising, I ask innocently, "Are you feeling unwell?"

He makes a sort of snarl, animalistic and dismissive. "The doctor tells me I haven't been properly taking my insulin. What does that moron know?"

Yes, I imagine graduating from medical school leaves a person totally ignorant of how the body works. Diabetes was a diagnosis Dimitri never fully came to accept, though he's had the disease as long as I've known him. It used to be my job to give him his daily injections. I wonder who's been doing it in my absence.

I wonder if anyone has.

Sweet Lord in heaven above, I hope not.

Without further comment on his condition, Dimitri turns to the priest, hands him two gold rings, and says, "Let's begin."

My blood turns to acid in my veins, and my panic comes crashing back with a vengeance, destroying my short moment of calm. This is wrong, all wrong, on so many levels. This can't really be happening. I'm in a nightmare, a terrible nightmare, and all I need to do now is wake myself up.

Wake up!

The priest, a heavily bearded old man in violet-and-gold embroidered vestments with an elaborate gold pectoral cross hanging halfway down his thin sternum, looks at me in alarm. He knows better than to mention my appearance, however, and quickly turns his gaze to the room, as if for help.

"The witnesses?"

Stefan steps forward, clearing his throat.

The priest knits his brows. "Only one?"

Dimitri's slow, aggravated exhalation doesn't leave room for argument about the number of witnesses.

Understanding this is not the usual wedding ceremony, and that Dimitri and I are not the usual bride and groom, the priest does his best to pretend this is all par for the course. *Yes, yes, it's every day that I join two people who look like survivors of a car crash together in a hastily arranged union with no friends or family present and the bride's hysteria hanging like fog over the room.*

Just another day in service of the Lord.

The priest begins by blessing the rings, praying over them and our betrothal as I stand there hyperventilating, my face drained of blood and my eyes filling with water. A wave is cresting over me, a tidal wave of anguish that threatens to sweep me under its cold current and hold me there, choking, until I drown.

The priest says, "Heavenly Father, bless these rings and this union with your sacred benediction. May you walk before this couple all the days of their lives, for you are the power that sanctifies all things."

He makes the sign of the cross, then holds out his hand, waiting for me to place my right hand in his so he can slip the ring on my third finger.

In a traditional Russian Orthodox wedding, it's the priest who puts the rings on the couple's hands during the betrothal. This is the first part of the ceremony, followed by the crowning and candle lighting, then drinking from the common cup, then more prayers and blessings. It's very elaborate and highly ritualized, steeped in symbolism and ancient tradition, but apparently we're doing the DIY home version, because the priest has skipped over the part where all parties are supposed to declare they've come freely, without constraint or prior commitment, to be joined before God. And there are no candles or crowns or cups.

I feel Dimitri watching me. I feel it when my heart stutters and throbs, and the exact moment it breaks.

My hand rises to meet the priest's, and it's shaking.

Naz. I love you. I'll love you until my dying breath.

"Oh," says a rumbling voice in Russian behind us. "I hope we're not interrupting."

We spin around to find a group of men crowding the entrance to the room.

They're all large, all imposing, all well dressed in expensive suits with fine wool or fur overcoats draped over wide shoulders. Hale and bearded to a one, they appear to range in age from forty to sixty, and they suffuse the room with a dangerous pulse of power.

The man who stands at the head of the group is the one who spoke, because he speaks again in the same whiskey deep rumble of a voice, his manner easy but his black eyes flashing.

"My invitation must've gotten lost in the mail."

He's the oldest of the group and also the most commanding. His russet beard is shot through with gray. He could pin you to a wall and hold you there simply with the force of his gaze. Each of his knuckles is tattooed with a different thing: skulls, letters, flowers.

I've seen those same tattoos somewhere before, but I can't remember where.

I'm too busy being terrified.

"Pakhan," says Dimitri, sounding surprised and not at all pleased. Then he swallows.

Swallows.

Behind us, the priest makes a noise like he's soiling his embroidered underwear.

Which is really the correct reaction when the godfather of the Russian Mafia makes a surprise appearance at your wedding, with all his captains in tow.

SEVENTEEN

EVA

Pakhan and his captains stroll into the room with unhurried ease, bringing with them the smell of rain and wet fur, cigars and aftershave, and that indefinable dark, edgy pheromone exuded by men who deal daily in violence.

I'm rooted to the spot, speechless with shock, stupid with fear. In all the years I lived with Dimitri in Russia, Pakhan never visited him. And now he's here? In Poland?

At our *wedding*?

Dimitri finds it as overwhelming as I do. Beside me, he smooths his hand over his hair, his unconscious grooming habit when he's agitated.

Pakhan stops a few feet away and regards Dimitri with an inscrutable look, a small smile playing at the corners of his mouth. He was handsome once, I think, but life—and all the death he's obviously seen—has made his features rugged and lined. Hardened, like igneous rock.

Not that it diminishes an ounce of his extraordinary power.

He offers his ringed hand to Dimitri, who bends and respectfully kisses it. When Dimitri rises, Pakhan casts a keen eye at me.

"You've been busy." An undercurrent of danger gives his words an edge.

Playing at calm, Dimitri says, "I would have invited you, of course, but we only recently reunited. I'm planning a party to celebrate with everyone in a month or so—"

"I wasn't talking about your wedding."

Pakhan's cold words stop Dimitri short. The tension in the room ratchets higher. Pakhan allows it to linger for a moment before saying more lightly, "Introduce me to your bride, Dimitri."

"Of course," Dimitri murmurs, obviously flustered. "Pakhan, this is Evalina. Evalina, this is—"

"I know who you are."

My interruption makes Pakhan raise his brows. His look sharpens. "Do you now?" In an aside to his men, he says, "My reputation precedes me."

Everyone chuckles, the sound like a nest of rattlesnakes shaking their tails.

I feel Dimitri's gaze on me, blisteringly hard, willing me to say nothing more or face his wrath, but I've caught the scent of the hunt, and I'm galloping hard toward a kill.

Because the fox who's being chased here isn't me.

So I stare directly at Pakhan when I say, "Yes. You're the one Dimitri calls the fat idiot."

Every man in the room falls perfectly still. Pakhan stares into my eyes, his small smile vanished. Gazing back at him is like staring into an abyss.

Behind me, the priest makes an audible whimper.

Dimitri's hand clamps down hard over my arm. "Forgive us, Pakhan," he hisses. "Of course that's not true. She's feeling unwell. As you can see, she's had a head injury."

Ignoring him, Pakhan turns to address Stefan. He's standing in the same spot he's been since we entered the room, off to one side, apart but engaged, his green eyes ablaze.

"Is this the one you spoke of?" Pakhan inquires, appearing genuinely confused.

Stefan nods.

"Is she simple?"

The question is a fair one. Whether true or not, only a complete simpleton—or someone with a death wish—would dare to utter those words to the godfather's face.

Or a woman with nothing left to lose.

Stefan turns his gaze to me. He says quietly, "No. She's lionhearted."

Dimitri looks sharply back and forth between us, realizing in a snap that not only do Stefan and I have more of a relationship than he understood, but so do Stefan and Pakhan.

Stefan is much more than a bodyguard: he's Pakhan's hired spy.

Dimitri's fury is palpable, a warpath rage screaming bloody murder inside him, screaming for scalps and vengeance, but all he can do is stand there, silent and impotent, and watch as everything falls apart.

Pakhan turns to regard me again, his bushy brows knitted and his eyes narrowed. "Lionhearted," he repeats thoughtfully, as if he likes the sound of it. He reaches out and brushes a rough knuckle across my cheek.

For a moment of sheer horror, I think I'll be upgrading from a Mafia prince to a Mafia king. But then Pakhan asks gently, "Tell me, beauty, what happened to your face?"

"Dimitri pistol-whipped me."

Aimed at his boss, Dimitri's defense comes fast and hard. "My women are mine to do with as I please."

Pakhan lightly cups my chin and turns my head to and fro, examining me as one would a gem under a jeweler's loupe or an expensive piece of art he was considering for purchase.

"Yes," he says, "but marring a face like this is like taking a sledgehammer to the *David*." Then, to me: "And your broken arm?"

"He pushed me down a staircase."

"Hmpf. Such foolish treatment of such a treasure."

He chucks me under the chin, like a grandfather would, then sends Dimitri a look of such terrifying intensity it would make me drop dead on the spot if it were directed at me.

"What other foolishness have you been up to, Dimitri?"

It's a trap, which Dimitri knows. His face goes white. His mouth opens and closes like a fish gasping for air. "I . . . I . . ."

Into Dimitri's stammering pause, Pakhan calmly supplies, "I what? I've been disloyal? I've embezzled money? I've attracted the attention of the police with all the bodies I've clumsily left lying around?"

"No—"

"No?" Pakhan's voice rises. "I suppose you also didn't use any of the money you embezzled from me to buy property all over this godforsaken country with a shell corporation in an attempt to hide it?"

Dimitri's sweating. His breathing has gone erratic. His throat works, as if he's trying not to swallow his own tongue.

Pakhan steps closer. "But finally, most importantly, I suppose you *didn't* make an arms deal that would've brought intense scrutiny on Russia if the weapon were deployed? Because of course whoever made that deal would have known that in the event of a nuclear strike, forensic scientists can identify where the weapon was built, regardless of where it was deployed from.

"And because whoever made the deal knew *that*, they also knew who the authorities in Russia would investigate first, considering my certain—how shall I put it?—prominence in the international black market arms industry. And in investigating me, they would've found some very *interesting* connections between myself and the Russian military, which is all they'd need to string me up by my neck."

Pakhan reaches out and adjusts Dimitri's lapels, smoothing one, wiping a stray piece of lint from the other. He continues in a thoughtful, pleasant tone.

"I wonder, since you had nothing to do with it, why we discovered a UR-100 warhead in the back of a lead-lined tractor trailer about to be offloaded to a cargo ship in the Gulf of Oman? And why both the tractor trailer and the cargo ship—through vigorous persuasion of many individuals, I won't bore you with the details—were traced directly back to . . . you?"

Dimitri stands stiff, hyperventilating, waiting for the ax he knows is going to fall.

Pakhan says softly, "You were attempting to usurp me."

Dimitri chokes out a half-strangled "I would *never*" before his words are cut off by Pakhan's sharp command.

"Take him!"

It happens so fast it's like a shark feeding frenzy.

One moment Dimitri is standing beside me, the next he's swarmed by a group of predators and dragged off, thrashing and screaming, into another room. The screaming intensifies briefly, then cuts off when it's overtaken by the sound of gunshots.

Three gunshots, to be precise.

With each one, the priest jumps and lets out a squeak of terror.

After a moment, the captains stroll leisurely back into the room as if coming in from a picnic. Hulking and malevolent, they line up behind Pakhan.

Then everyone looks at me.

So does Pakhan, who clasps his hands at his waist and says, "Now, what are we going to do with *you*?"

Overwhelmed, the priest takes the opportunity to faint. He crumples to the floor and lies there unmoving, or possibly dead.

Perhaps even more than Dimitri's sudden demise, I'm stunned by hearing that Pakhan has the missing nuke. And judging from his opinion that all fingers would be pointed in his direction if it were ever deployed, it seems the nuke is going to *stay* missing.

So another silver lining. Even if I'm about to have my face blown off, Venezuela will never get their weapon, and millions of Floridians will continue to live peacefully in blanket-thick humidity and work on their tans.

As if from very far away, I hear myself say, "You're going to let me go and live my life."

The captains think that's funny. They chuckle, sending each other knowing glances, shaking their heads. But Pakhan simply looks at me.

"And why would I do that, beauty? What've you got to live for?"

Either he's a cat, batting at a toy, or he's actually weighing my fate. Considering.

I know too much. I've seen too much firsthand, including this, a wedding-day execution. As far as he's concerned, I probably have all kinds of damning evidence I could share with the police, if I had a mind to.

So whatever words I speak have to be compelling enough to make the scales tip over to my side.

Incongruous but urgent, a movie scene pops into my head. It's from *The Princess Bride*, a movie Naz and I often quoted to each other, a fairy tale about a boy who loved a girl so much he successfully begged for his life from the pirate who wanted to kill him by saying two words. Two simple words that spun the wheel of fate in a different direction. Two simple words of truth.

My eyes filling with tears, I whisper, "True love."

Pakhan's expression sours. He turns again to Stefan. "She's definitely simple."

"No." Stefan steps forward, coming to stand next to me. He faces Pakhan with respect but no sign of fear. He says, "She's pregnant. It's not Dimitri's."

A ripple of surprise goes through the group of men.

Stefan goes on. "Dimitri killed the father of the child. In Vienna, that apartment thing. Then he kidnapped her and brought her here."

Understanding dawns over Pakhan's rugged features. He obviously already knew about what happened in Vienna, but not why until right now.

The following silence is the longest I've endured in my life. I see the wheels turning behind Pakhan's eyes, see all his men impatient to get it over with and dispose of the pregnant lady so they can go get an early supper.

When the silence stretches on too long, Stefan says, "I'll vouch for her."

This statement is met with blinking disbelief from everyone but Pakhan, who has begun to consider me with an expression of—if not quite outright admiration for my intellect—slightly less contempt.

"So will I," says a timid voice behind the men.

Everyone turns. Astrid, the gray-haired kitchen maid, stands in the corridor beside the mute maid, whose name no one ever told me. They're clinging to one another in obvious terror, knowing who these men are and what they've just done, but standing straight, their quivering chins lifted.

Their courage astonishes me.

Fingers flashing, the mute maid says something in sign language to Astrid, who interprets. "So will Nadja." She gestures to me. "This woman was a victim of Dimitri's, not his partner, and kind to us both."

One of the captains rolls his eyes. "Maids can't vouch for anyone."

"And I'm not a victim," I say, overly loud.

Everyone turns back to me, but I address Pakhan alone, in one final, last-ditch effort to save myself and my baby.

I'll be my own goddamn knight in shining armor.

"At least I won't be if you let me go. If I pay the price in blood for Dimitri's sins, a victim is what I'll be reduced to. That's what he would have wanted for me, what he tried to make me. He tried to take everything away from me. My voice. My freedom. My self-respect. He wanted me to grovel for him, to worship him, and I wouldn't. But if you . . . if you decide . . ."

I stop for a moment to inhale a ragged breath before I go on. "If you decide that I—*we*—should die with him, then he wins." My voice grows hard with hatred. "And that pathetic bastard doesn't deserve to win anything."

In the beat before Pakhan smiles, universes are born and die and are reborn from the ashes. Then he chuckles. "It's too bad you're not a man. I could've used someone like you in the ranks."

Which, as far as compliments from Mafia godfathers go, is about as extravagant as it gets.

He turns serious, drawing himself up to his full, imposing height. "Tell me your full name."

"Evalina Nikolaevna Petrovna."

I don't hesitate, fearing any pause will be taken for disrespect. Though it's been years since I told someone my real surname—I'd been forced to use Dimitri's for so long—it feels completely natural. A sweet relief from restriction, like when a snake sheds its skin.

"Where are your people from?"

"Kirishi." I still don't hesitate, though I have no idea where he's going with this.

He nods, passing a hand over his beard. "I've been to Kirishi. What a shithole."

"Yes. My family was poor."

He's dismissive of that historical nugget. "Meh. So was mine. Poverty separates the strong from the weak. If you can survive it, you're unbreakable. Your parents are alive?"

"No. They both passed."

"So your father was Nikolai Petrov. Your mother's name?"

This is getting stranger and stranger, but I know there's a purpose soon to be revealed. "Sofia."

He considers me for a moment in thoughtful silence, stroking his beard. Then he nods to himself, as if he's made a decision.

"All right, Evalina Nikolaevna, little lionhearted beauty. Go live your life. But I know your face and one or two things about you. Now I can find out anything about you."

He pauses to let that sink in. I stand still and wait, not daring to breathe.

"Get out of Poland. Don't go back to Russia. Don't contact anyone you knew before this moment. Your past is dead." His gaze intensifies. "And don't let me hear even a whisper about you ever again. You'll vanish, or I'll forget I was in a good humor today. Understand?"

It's a threat, and not a subtle one. If he orders murders of his men in good humor, I'd hate to see what his temper looks like. "Yes," I whisper, trying desperately not to keel over. "Thank you, Pakhan."

He chucks me under the chin again. I think he enjoys the contrast between that homey, grandfatherly gesture and, well, what he is.

"Everything in this house belongs to me, but you're welcome to those jewels," he adds, eyeing my necklace. "I'm sure they'll get you anywhere you want to go. Stefan, take care of the body."

"With pleasure, sir."

Pakhan turns and walks out, taking all his captains with him.

⌘

I'm wearing the same jeans and T-shirt I wore when I arrived at the manor when I leave it.

The shoes are new, taken from the closet of the bridal suite, a pair of butter-soft leather driving moccasins that were surely an ironic purchase by Dimitri, as he never allowed me to drive. Everything else I left untouched, per Pakhan's instructions.

I doubt he had an inventory of the place, but you never know, and I'm not taking any chances. I've got more than my own safety to think of from now on.

Astrid and Nadja—or any of the rest of the staff, for that matter—are nowhere to be seen when Stefan finishes doing whatever he did with Dimitri's body and comes into my room, offering to give me a ride into the city.

"The city?" I repeat, confused.

He glances at the diamonds, still sparkling around my neck. "You'll need to fence those for cash. I know a place."

When we pass the dining room as we leave, the missing staff are all gathered around the long marble table, standing, hurriedly eating what looks like a catered meal. On the sideboard sits a tiered frosted cake decorated with sugar flowers that no one has touched.

It's probably bad luck to eat a wedding cake when the groom was shot halfway through the ceremony.

Everyone stops and looks at me for a moment. Then someone says quietly, *"Geh mit gott."*

Go with God.

It's Astrid, at the end of the table next to Nadja, who puts her hand over her heart and nods, seconding the sentiment.

I don't want to cry, but I can't help it. The tears are already coming, cresting over my bottom lids and sliding down my cheeks. In German, I tell her, "You too, friend. You too."

Then Stefan tugs my arm, and we go out into the storm.

On the drive into the city, we're silent. There's nothing to say. Stefan's fence gives me a good price for the diamonds, enough so I won't have to worry about money until long after I'm finished with all the therapy I'm going to need.

Then we're back in the car with the rain drumming hard on the roof and the beginnings of my new companion hysteria turning my vision dark around the edges, as dark as the evening sky.

"Where to?" asks Stefan, sticking the keys into the ignition.

"I . . . I don't know. I don't have anywhere to go."

I want to find out what happened to Naz after the police found him in Vienna, what they're doing with his body, where he'll be buried. I want to call Tabby and Connor and cry with them, thank them for all they did for us, tell them what happened and why. And Killian, too. He tried to help us, even though he made Naz want to tear out his hair.

I desperately, so desperately want to say proper goodbyes, but I know if I do, I run the risk of Pakhan finding out.

"Vanish," he said. *"Don't contact anyone you knew."*

He has eyes and ears everywhere. Russia is out of the question, but if I go back to Vienna to make inquiries about Naz, surely someone will hear about that. There were witnesses in Vienna. All those neighbors who gathered in whispering groups and watched as I was thrown into a van.

The police will be looking for that woman. They'll be looking for me.

So Vienna is out of the question, also . . . and so, I realize with sinking regret, are goodbyes.

Because there's a better than good chance that Pakhan will make anyone I might contact vanish, too. Loose ends aren't tolerated in the Bratva. Loose ends are tied into a noose.

And Stefan vouched for me, so his neck would be in a noose, too.

Stefan reaches out and touches my leg. I jump, startled from my thoughts, and look over at him.

"Go somewhere that will make you happy," he says gently, his eyes soft. "Somewhere warm, maybe. Somewhere pretty. Go raise your baby and don't look back. Don't regret. The past can only imprison you if you let it."

I clasp his rough hand and draw a heavy breath, struggling for words through all the emotions gnawing at me. The shock and elation, the disbelief and the sorrow, the anguish and rage and bone-scraping, chest-hollowing grief. I'm a basket of contradictions, everything writhing around in too small a space.

"I want to thank you," I start hesitantly, not sure if I can find the right words for something so huge. "For what you did for me. For vouching for me like that. I . . . I think if you hadn't, I wouldn't be sitting here. I think I owe my life to you."

Our lives. I'm still reeling too much to say it aloud.

He squeezes my hand. "You tried to protect Vova. I don't know of anyone else who would've had the courage to do that. Not even me." He gazes down at our joined hands, his face twisted with shame.

Hearing how tenderly this big, dangerous man says his nickname for Vlad, how he so obviously is crucifying himself over not saving him, perhaps also over never telling him how he felt before it was too late, makes me want to cry again. I swipe angrily at my watering eyes, wondering how many years it will be before they'll dry.

"I'm glad you were able to contact Killian and get the information about the nuke for Pakhan."

"I didn't contact him. I tried calling him six times but only got an answering service. I left messages, but he never called me back."

Stunned isn't a strong enough word for the emotion that grips me. "But then how did Pakhan know?"

"I don't know. I wasn't the one who told him about the shell corporation, either, but someone obviously had ample proof of both." He shrugs. "Pakhan has ways of finding things out on his own."

Why wouldn't Killian return Stefan's call? That makes no sense. He wanted that nuke just as badly as everyone else did. Was it Tabby? She's capable of finding anything out about anybody, but how would she know to warn Pakhan? How would she know Dimitri obtained the nuke without his permission?

I don't understand what happened, what circumstances led to this, but Stefan's explanation must be right. Pakhan has his ways. He didn't become the most powerful man in Russia for nothing.

Then something else Stefan said strikes me, and suddenly I know where I want to go.

Somewhere warm. Somewhere pretty. Somewhere I can leave the past behind.

I know of only one place like that. The place I left my past behind for one brief, beautiful moment in time.

The only place in the world where I was ever truly happy.

I look out the windshield into the raging storm and promise myself that someday, somehow, I'll find out where Naz is buried. When our child is old enough to hear the story, I'll tell her about her father—her kind, smart, funny as hell father—and I'll take her to visit his grave.

But in the meantime, I've got vanishing to do.

And I know just where I'm going to do it.

I turn back to Stefan. "Do you happen to know anyone who can get me a fake ID and a passport on short notice?"

As an answer, he guns the engine and smiles.

EIGHTEEN

NAZ

Flying a helicopter through a lightning storm isn't as bad an idea as it might at first sound.

Like a plane's, a helicopter's aluminum skin is designed to conduct electricity around it and not through it, giving protection to the people inside. You'll get a helluva bang and a bright flash if the bird is struck, maybe a hole in a tail rotor blade where the electricity exits and damage to the radio or avionics equipment from the surge, but the bird should still be able to land.

So no, it's not the chance of getting struck by lightning that's the real problem when flying in a storm.

It's the fucking *wind*.

"Hell's bells," mutters the pilot over the com as we hit yet another severe downdraft. Jolting to the side, the metal cage around us shuddering, the bird dives a few hundred feet in altitude in seconds.

My stomach dives with it. My shoulders ram against the harness for the umpteenth time. The pilot struggles for a moment until he's able to bring the bird back up to altitude and level off, but my heart keeps banging around inside my chest for a lot longer than that.

For an airplane, a few-hundred-foot drop is no biggie. For a helicopter, however, which typically flies at altitudes less than a thousand feet, it is.

The treetops are right beneath us. Another drag of wind shear and we could get driven into the ground before the pilot has a chance to correct.

To distract myself from the high possibility of imminent death, I make a list of all the things I'm going to do when I find Eva.

1. Kill Dimitri
2. Kiss her and tell her I love her
3. Kill everyone else

That's as far as I get before the pilot says, "Four klicks to the LZ."

The landing zone is another country field near our final destination. We've been at this all day, starting with the flight from Vienna to Kraków, where we had to refuel. The entire country of Poland is blanketed with severe weather, with clouds too thick for satellite imaging to penetrate.

It's a big *fuck you* from the elements, because not only have we had to delay takeoffs when the weather was too bad to fly, but Tabby and Connor couldn't get eyes on our targets from above to discover anything that might be useful about what I'd be walking into.

From below—just for some extra fuckery—a bunch of electrical grids have been taken out by severe wind and cascading failures on the power network.

So not only are we flying in the wind, we're flying in the dark, too.

Not that any of it could stop me. I'll crawl there on my hands and knees if I have to.

When we get to the field, it looks like a rippling black lake beneath us. The landing is awkward and hard, a bone-cracking jolt that sends waves of water spraying up into the rotors.

Before I remove my headphones, the driver shouts, "I won't be able to take off in this cheeser. We're grounded again until the storm lightens up."

I want to swear at him, but he's already doing me a huge favor.

It was Doc who arranged for this guy to take me out, some friend of his who flies him where he needs to go last minute. He speaks perfect English with no accent, but it's a touch too formal and sprinkled with old-timey words to be his first language, like he taught himself from watching black-and-white movies on TV.

I don't know his name. Doc simply called him "the pilot," and the man himself didn't offer it up, so I'm guessing everyone in Doc and Killian's circle just goes by their job title.

Doc. Pilot. Annoying Spy.

"Copy that." I unhook the harness belt and slide it off my shoulders, then grab my rucksack and rifle, flip down my night-vision goggles, and jump out into boot-sucking mud.

Ignoring it, I turn the NVGs on and head east toward the stand of ghostly green-lit trees, my ruck on my back and my rifle gripped in my hands. I know from studying a map of the terrain that beyond the trees is a hill, and beyond the hill is my destination. But it's still more than a one-kilometer hump in pissing rain loaded with heavy gear, and it's gonna take a while.

My injuries don't help. At this point, I'm running on nothing but fumes and desperation. If Eva isn't here—

Focus on the mission, soldier!

"I hear ya, Master Sergeant McCall," I mutter, and break into a trot, pushing my worries aside.

It's times like these I'm grateful I have the ghost of that old bastard who made my days in the corps a living hell still hanging out in my head.

The goggles are good quality and don't blind me when lightning burns jagged fingers of white fire across the sky. Another favor from

Doc, along with all the gear, even the rifle. I suppose it all technically belongs to Killian, but I'm too pissed off at him to be thankful.

He didn't respond to any of Doc's attempts to reach him before I left. Wherever he is and whatever he's doing, he obviously wants to be off the grid.

I break the tree line and push ahead, trudging through sucking mud and thick undergrowth, the rising slope slippery with scree and almost impossible to keep my footing in. I go down hard on my knees a bunch of times. My stomach growls. My lungs burn. The sewn-up gash in my calf screams, and the one in my gut feels like it's leaking. With all the miles of terrain I've covered today, I've probably torn my stitches.

Beyond the thick stand of pines looms an imposing hill, rising high enough to block out a substantial portion of the thunderclouds. I knew the elevation from studying a map before I left, but looking at it from the ground after a full day's freezing slog on an empty stomach around what seems like every goddamn swampy, remote country field in Poland makes me want to shoot something.

Instead, I forge ahead.

At the crest of the hill, I slow and sink into a crouch, still moving forward but more carefully, sweeping the blackness ahead for any sign of warm bodies. The terrain has changed to scrub and stunted trees, less easy to be camouflaged by, though the night is as black as pitch.

I don't know if Dimitri's had time to install the kind of security systems he has on his home in Saint Petersburg on this property I'm approaching, but if nothing else, he'll have men patrolling the perimeter of the grounds.

If he's here, that is. *If* this property even belongs to him. All the other mansions I surveilled today were empty. Some furnished, some not, and some that looked downright abandoned, but all devoid of life.

There's a glow just ahead that tells me this one will be different.

I crawl the last few yards on my belly, finding a partially sheltered spot under the boughs of a gnarled larch, and peer through my night-vision goggles at the small valley spread out below.

When I spot the estate, adrenaline crackles through me.

Lit up like a Christmas tree, it's spread over thousands of square feet, huge and glowing white. It sports balconies on the third floor, formal gardens in the back, a large circular drive in the front, and is surrounded by acres of parklike plantings. *Palatial* is the word that comes to mind. It must be powered by generators, because everything else in the surrounding grid is dark.

I lie still, looking and listening, my blood pounding through my veins and my skin feeling tight as rain pours over me in sheets.

I'm coming, sweetheart. Hang on a little longer. Your Beastie is coming for you.

After about ten minutes, I haven't seen a single bodyguard on patrol or any movement from within the estate. Some of the windows have their shades drawn, but a surprising amount of them are open to the night, allowing prying eyes to easily see in.

Both the lack of guards and the uncovered windows bother me. A man as paranoid as Dimitri wouldn't leave himself so vulnerable. If it belongs to him, this place should be crawling with armed men and locked up tighter than a chastity belt.

My thoughts are interrupted by headlights sweeping through the darkness to the south. A car appears far back on a winding country road, moving with caution through the rain as it heads toward the house.

I leap to my feet and break into a flat-out sprint, pumping my legs as fast as they'll take me.

Reaching the road as the car crests a low rise, I skid to a halt, flip up the NVGs, and raise my rifle. Training the sights on the driver, I stand with my legs spread as the car comes to an abrupt stop several meters away, its wheels spitting gravel.

The man—Caucasian, thirtyish, bearded—appears to be alone in the car. His hands are in full view, gripped around the steering wheel, and he makes no attempt to move or reach for a gun. His expression doesn't register surprise or fear, only a weird sort of confusion.

He stares at me with his brows drawn together and his eyes narrowed, as if trying to place where he's seen me before.

Or maybe it's simple annoyance. If he works for Dimitri, he's probably used to having guns pointed at his face.

I approach the car slowly, every nerve on screaming high alert, my trigger finger itchy. My gaze darts everywhere as I wait for any movement from the back seat or the driver, anticipating he'll lunge for a weapon at any moment.

That moment never comes. I find myself standing next to the driver's window without incident. The entire time I'm carefully edging toward the car, he simply sits there and looks at me.

I know this isn't just some local dude out for a scenic drive in the middle of a raging storm on the only road leading in and out of this gargantuan estate. He's got some business here, whatever it is. But his eerie calm at having an armed man in full combat fatigues and body armor approach him borders on unnerving.

I shout, "Get out of the car!"

He nods to acknowledge the command, then lifts his hands slowly from the wheel and shows them to me, palms up, to indicate he's unarmed. He points at the door handle with a question in his gaze, wanting permission to reach for it.

I nod, stepping back a few paces and training my weapon on the center of his chest as he exits the car.

His dark hair and tight white button-down dress shirt are drenched in seconds. He stands beside the open door, hands up, breath steaming in the freezing rain, and stares at me in utter stillness.

Recognition dawns over his features. In English, he says, *"You."*

I'm about to shoot him, just because he's freaking me the fuck out, but then—*holy shit*—I realize I know him from the intel Tabby sent.

This is the guy we discovered from Vlad's phone. The ex-military commander turned bodyguard for bad guys.

My voice comes out in an animal's snarl. "Stefan. Where's Dimitri?"

He blinks when I say his name, the first time he's shown anything even close to surprise. "How do you know me?"

I snap back, "How do you know *me*?"

"Your obituary."

He saw the article in the newspaper. My heart thuds, flops, skips a beat. In three long strides, I've got the barrel of the rifle shoved into his sternum.

"Where's Dimitri?"

"Dead."

I'm so shocked by that response I almost accidentally pull the trigger and blow a hole clean through his chest. Instead, I jerk back and stare at him.

"Bullshit."

He points toward the house. "I'll show you the body if you want. I put him in a plastic drum and submerged him in sodium hydroxide. His bones are boiling to sludge as we speak."

I'm dubious. "Just happened to have a plastic drum and a few jugs of sodium hydroxide lying around, did you?"

He shrugs. "You'd be surprised how often someone tells me to get rid of a body."

It's my turn to narrow my eyes. "You don't seem really torn up about having to dissolve your boss."

"He was a worthless piece of shit who deserved what he got. Actually, he deserved worse than he got. It was over too quick for my liking."

There's a hardness in his tone and his eyes, a certain swell of emotion you can't fake that tells me he's being honest. I don't know what to make of it. The only thing I know for sure is I have a million questions, and I don't want to ask them standing out in the pouring rain.

I jerk my chin at the trunk. "Open it."

"It opens with a button on the key."

Which means either he has to go back into the car, shut it off, and take out the key—along with possibly taking out a stashed weapon—or I've got to do it and turn my back on him in the process.

I step back a foot and point the rifle at his face. "One wrong move and you'll be joining Dimitri in that drum."

He nods, then, letting me see his hands, eases into the car and switches off the engine. He pops the trunk, then gets out of the car and stands there with his hands raised as I slowly walk backward, keeping one eye on him and the other on the trunk.

It's empty.

I slam it shut, do another quick scan of the interior to confirm there's no one hiding on the floor in back, then tell him to turn around and put his hands on the roof.

He does it without a word of debate or an ounce of resistance.

I frisk him, expecting at any moment he'll whip out a knife and try to stab me in the eye, but that's another expected moment that doesn't come. He stands still and relaxed as I run my hands over him. I find a revolver strapped to his ankle and another one in the waistband of his trousers, and I toss both of them away, wondering why in the hell he isn't trying to take me out.

It's one thing to hate the guy you were assigned to spy on. It's another thing to be an ex-military badass strapped with weapons acting as docile as a little lamby lamb when another ex-military badass strapped with weapons frisks and disarms you on a deserted country road after threatening your life.

And the way he stands there with his eyes closed and his mouth lax as I roughly search him . . . it's almost like he likes it.

"Get in."

He obeys me, sitting in the driver's seat with his hands resting lightly on the wheel. Keeping a careful eye on him, I toss my ruck and rifle into the back seat, remove a sidearm from a pocket of my tactical vest, then get into the passenger seat and point it at him.

"No sudden moves or I'll liquefy your brains. Close your door."

He swings it shut, then rests his hands on the steering wheel again and waits patiently for my next instruction.

Either this fucker is nuts or he's got balls of steel.

"How many guards are at the house?"

"There were twelve when I left, but they'll be gone by now, along with the rest of the staff."

"Gone? Why?"

Dripping wet, he turns his head and peers at me through the dark interior. The rain sounds like a hail of bullets on the roof. "When a captain is killed for disloyalty, his staff won't take a chance that they'll be found complicit. Nobody hangs around to see if Pakhan will find them another job."

"Pakhan?"

"The boss of all bosses. The one you don't want to cross."

"Why are you going back, then?"

"Because I worked for him. Keeping an eye on Dimitri, reporting back."

Christ. Another spy. I'm up to my neck in these assholes. "So this Pakhan killed Dimitri?"

"Yes. Well, the other captains did, on Pakhan's orders."

Not Eva, then. For some strange reason, that's a relief. I know she wanted to kill him something fierce, but I also know taking a life would weigh on her conscience, no matter how evil that particular life was. "Did Dimitri have a woman with him here?"

When he's silent too long, I prompt, "Brunette. Big brown eyes. Beautiful as fuck."

He looks like he's trying to decide whether or not to tell me something, so I give him a little nudge in the right direction and stick my gun into the space between his brows.

It unlocks his memory. "You mean Evalina."

The emotions that blast through me at hearing him speak her name are beyond description. The gun in my hand starts to shake. "Where is she?"

"Now? I don't know."

"Did Pakhan take her?" *Please, God, say no.*

I hold my breath until he says, "No."

Oh Jesus. Sweet Mother Mary. Breathe, Naz. Just breathe. For one split second, I'm drenched in relief, but that turns right back into the indescribable boiling cauldron of emotion when I realize there's something worse this Pakhan person could've done.

"Did he . . ."

Sounding relieved himself, Stefan says, "No. He let her go."

I take a moment to get my ragged breathing under control before I ask, "Go? Go where? Where is she?"

"I told you. I don't know."

He seems like he's telling the truth, but I have to make sure she's not at the manor, injured or worse. As long as she's still out there somewhere, breathing, I can find her, but first I have to confirm she's not here.

"Okay, spy. Drive up to the house. *Slowly.*"

He puts the car in gear and steps on the gas. We trundle over the gravel road, crawling along in silence interrupted only by the occasional bass boom of thunder from above. When we reach the main driveway, we take a turn and follow it around to the side of the house and the bank of garages.

Stefan says, "I'm going to open that one on the end with the remote. It's clipped to the visor. Don't shoot me."

He glances at me to make sure he's good to go before reaching up and jabbing a finger into a button on the small black remote. A door at the end of the bank slides up on rollers, opening to reveal a big, tidy, lighted space. As we pull in, I glimpse a lineup of exotic cars to our left, along with floor-to-ceiling built-in cabinetry.

Next to the cabinetry lurks a row of tall blue plastic drums the size of garbage cans, only more industrial and *way* more creepy looking.

We pull to a stop. Stefan asks, "Should I turn it off?"

"Yeah. Then I'm gonna get out and you're gonna sit tight."

He kills the engine, then sets his hands back on the steering wheel and stares straight ahead. I get the sense he's waiting for me to do something, only I don't know what. Shoot him? Knock him out? Ask him more questions?

All of the above are on the table, I want to say, but instead I jump out of the car, round the back, and point my sidearm at him through the window. "Out you come."

He steps out, shutting the door behind him, dripping water all over the epoxy floor. He gives me a thorough once-over, head to toe, his sharp gaze cataloging every detail of my appearance.

Then, just to throw me for a complete fucking loop, he says—with a totally *straight face*—"You're very photogenic, but you're much better looking in person."

I do one of those comical double takes, blinking and shaking my head. "Uh . . ."

"It's those exotic cheekbones, I think. And those thighs—you must work out a lot. Would you like me to show you Dimitri now?"

He lifts a calm hand toward the row of plastic drums, as if he hasn't just dropped a grenade in my lap.

My thighs?

I pause to compose myself, because I'm a grown man, a professional, and have a mission to complete. If this guy thinks I'm cute, well, I'll just have to deal with it.

"Yes."

He turns and walks casually to one of the cabinets, opens it, pulls out a chemical mask, a rubber apron, and thick rubber gloves, then puts them all on. He hands me a mask, too.

"For the fumes," he explains, as if we're touring a factory.

When he removes a metal crowbar from the cabinet, I snap into high-alert mode, but he ignores me, instead walking over to one of the drums and prying off the thick lid. He steps back to allow me to approach, but even from feet away I recognize what's inside.

Though the skin of his face has dissolved, leaving the underlying muscle and bones showing through, I can tell it's Dimitri.

Then the smell hits me. The overripe slaughterhouse carrion stench.

I slap the mask over my face and wave the gun at Stefan to make him put the cover back on.

He does, quickly and efficiently, then takes off the protective gear and puts everything away neatly in the cabinet. "I assume you'll want to look through the house to make sure she isn't here?"

This is going way too smoothly for my liking. I toss the mask aside and say, "Turn around."

When he complies, I grab him by his collar and shove my gun into the small of his back. "You're gonna lead the way. Anyone we find's gonna get a bullet. You do anything stupid, you're gonna get a bullet. Deal?"

"Deal," he says promptly. "Unless Astrid and Nadja are still here. You don't want to shoot them. They're very nice."

I don't bother asking him who the fuck Astrid and Nadja are. I just push him forward, shaking my head.

It takes a while for us to roam from room to room because the place is so big. We don't encounter anyone, and I see and hear nothing to indicate people are anywhere inside. When we enter a huge all-white suite, I stop him inside the doorway, staring in surprise at the mess.

It looks like someone let a rabid wolverine loose.

We wind through smashed vases, kicked-over tables and chairs, and destroyed artwork until we enter a bathroom. Inside the adjoining closet, jewel-tone dresses are strewn in tangled piles all over the floor. The faintest hint of jasmine perfumes the air.

My skin prickles in recognition. "This was Eva's room."

"Yes." After a moment, Stefan adds, "Dimitri didn't sleep here."

I think he's trying to make me feel better. What I feel, however, can't be made better by anything in heaven or on earth. Bile is already rising up the back of my throat at the thought of what he might have done to Eva. The thought of how many hours he had alone with her to satisfy his every perverted, evil need.

"He was injured, also."

Stefan's voice jolts me out of my thoughts. I say gruffly, "What?"

"Dimitri. When they got here, he'd been shot in the stomach. I assume that was your doing? The gunfight at the apartment in Vienna? Anyway, he wouldn't go to a hospital to have it treated. Eva said it was because he was too paranoid, and that he thought he was a god. She was right about both, but my point is that I don't think . . ."

He searches for words for a moment before going on. "The wound became infected quickly. He was in a lot of pain."

What he's trying to politely tell me is that he doesn't think Dimitri could sexually perform.

I grab his shoulder and force him to face me, then rest the barrel of the gun at the base of his throat. We're about the same height, so we stand eye to eye. "What else?" I demand.

When he lifts his brows, I raise my voice. "It sounds like you knew everything that went on here. What else happened?"

He studies my face carefully. After a moment, he says, "I've led countless men. In battle, in business, in life. I haven't known one of her equal. What happened here is that your woman gave me a lesson in endurance under pressure. She gave me a lesson in doing the right thing, even though it might cost everything. She gave me a lesson in what grit really looks like."

"Jesus Christ," I say, my voice shaking. "What the hell did he do to her?"

"You're missing my point."

I lose it and start shouting. *"Then what the fuck is your fucking point?"*

"Stop worrying about what already happened and focus on what's important."

That little piece of advice infuriates me so much I shove him against the wall and make him acquainted with the strength of my left hand by clamping it around his throat.

Teeth bared, I growl at him, "Stop playing games with me. Whatever it is I need to know, say it. *Right now*, or so help me God you won't live long enough to draw another breath."

As an answer, he simply sends a pointed glance to his right.

I follow his gaze. He's looking at the bathroom counter, a long stretch of gleaming white marble interrupted by double sinks. "What? What're you looking at?"

He points at a small pink cardboard box by the sink near our end. It's torn open on one end. A piece of folded white paper sticks out of the glued flaps.

"What the fuck is that?"

"Oh. You can't read Polish?"

My hand clamps down tighter around his throat.

His voice strangled, he says, "It's a pregnancy test."

Time stops. My heart stops. The earth stops spinning.

I release him, stumble back several feet, then look back and forth between him and the little pink box with the gun lowered at my side and my whole body shaking.

He coughs, drags in a few ragged breaths, clears his throat. "It was positive, in case you're wondering."

His tone is sarcastic. I'd shoot him, but I'm too stunned to coordinate the effort it would take to pull a trigger. *Pregnant. Eva's pregnant . . . oh God.*

Everything's coming at me at once. Emotions, memories, hot and cold flashes, a sudden and almost overpowering urge to weep. Stefan sees my helplessness and sighs.

"Okay, tough guy. I'm going to help you out here, but only because I know she would have wanted me to."

Dazed, I blink at him.

"Ask me where I was coming back from when you stopped me on the road."

I lick my lips. My mouth is so dry I'm not sure I'll be able to speak, but I just manage it. "Where were you coming back from?"

He smiles. "From getting new ID and traveling papers for my friend, Thelma N. Dudley. I don't know where she's headed, but I do know the name she'll use to get there."

Thelma and Dudley. Our fake names from Cozumel.

I think I might be about to faint.

Instead, I grab Stefan in a rib-crushing bear hug and rasp, "Thank you. Oh fuck. Oh God. Thank you so much."

He pats me on the back. "You're welcome. Now please release me, unless you enjoy the feel of another man's erection against your big muscular thigh."

I pull away from him, misty eyed and grinning. "Brother, in this case, it would almost be worth it." When he arches a brow, a frisky gleam in his green eyes, I emphasize, *"Almost."*

I bolt out the door, leaving the sound of his chuckles fading fast behind me.

NINETEEN

Eva

Mexico.

Beautiful land of waving palms and sunny skies, of tropical breezes and friendly smiles, of ancient temples, pristine beaches, and humid rain forests teeming with life. A paradise for everyone who lives and visits there.

But especially for those who need to get lost and stay that way.

I picked Los Cabos for its rugged coastal beauty, but also for its popularity with tourists. Thousands of new faces come and go every week, a transient tide that provides a lovely veil of anonymity. In a smaller town, I'd be conspicuous. Newcomers are noticed. New faces are met with curiosity or distrust. But in a place where people constantly flow in and out like commuters through subway turnstiles, no one notices anything. No one stands out.

No one cares who you are, where you came from, or how much of your heart you left behind.

In the week since I arrived, the only thing of significance I've done is rent an apartment. It came furnished, with clean but worn furniture and a gorgeous view of the sea. The ancient fridge has no freezer. Air-conditioning is provided by opening the two rusted windows on opposite sides of the living room. But it has everything I need, and best of all, it's all mine.

Ours. Mine and Baby Beastie's, who's doing his or her best to make me puke up my entire intestinal tract every single day.

I'm standing in front of a display of brilliant red chili peppers at the local outdoor market when a wave of nausea hits me. I press my hand over my stomach and blow out a breath, closing my eyes to counteract the way the market stall has started to spin.

Oh, that was another thing of significance I did: visited a doctor. She confirmed what the plastic stick had already foretold and started me on prenatal vitamins. I'll go back to her in the next few weeks to have the cast on my arm removed.

When she wondered how I broke it, I asked her if it really mattered. She paused for a moment, looking at the stitches in my cheek, then asked me quietly if I wanted to make a report to the police.

"Don't worry about it. It's already been taken care of."

I think my smile unsettled her. She cleared out of the exam room pretty fast after that.

"*¿Estás bien, señorita?*"

The old woman who owns the vegetable stall has skin the color of saddle leather and a wide, gap-toothed grin. At the moment, however, her usual grin has been replaced by a look of concern. I've visited her stall nearly every day since I arrived here and have grown to like her. She always gives me something small for free, patting my hand and clucking her tongue.

Like the doctor, she clearly has her suspicions about the origins of my cast and stitches. I'm a little worried that I've begun to exude an air of flinching fear, like a dog that's been kicked too much.

"*Estoy bien, gracias.*"

I'm well. A lie, but a white one. I can hardly tell this lovely woman the ugly truth, that I'm pregnant by my dead lover who was murdered by the Mafia prince who kept me as a slave for seven years, who was then murdered by his boss in the middle of our shotgun wedding.

Her elderly heart wouldn't be able to take it. Mine is decades younger, and it's barely managing.

She glances at my hand pressed over my belly. Her grin returns. She says something in Spanish, cackling, then holds up a finger, turns around, and totters off to the back of her stall. Rummaging around through some small wooden crates, she finds whatever she's looking for, then returns to me, holding out her hand.

She dumps a gnarled piece of gingerroot into my palm. Gesturing with her hands, she indicates I'm supposed to slice it up and eat it to help with my nausea.

"Oh, how sweet of you. *Muchas gracias, señora.*"

She beams at me. I beam back at her.

It's then, sharing a smile with a kind stranger, that I feel it.

At first it's a prickle. A delicate current of electricity skittering across my skin that has all the tiny hairs on the back of my neck standing on end. The little prickle quickly blooms into a full-body frisson of chills and shivers sounding an alarm in the deepest pit of my brain, that ancient part of the cerebellum that existed long before we were creatures who could reason or speak. That hardwired alarm system that helped us survive when we were nothing more than pack animals of keen senses and brutality, lifting our noses to scent approaching danger in the dark.

It's instinct. Awareness. A sudden undeniable *knowing*.

And what the animal that lives beneath my skin is howling is that somewhere nearby, someone is looking at me.

Looking *hard*.

My pulse quickens, as does my breath, but I don't outwardly react. I simply pay for my bag of vegetables and turn around, scanning the crowded market with forced calm.

I see nothing and no one unusual. The sunny square ringed with vendors is thronged with people shopping and chatting, eating and smoking, sipping coffee in the shade of colorful umbrellas. Mariachi music plays on a tinny radio. Laughing children chase each other over the cobblestones. The smell of spiced roasting meat and salt water wafts through the air.

Everything looks normal, but still it's there, the ancient alarm bell, ringing in my head and stomach, warning me of a predator.

I curse my lack of a gun, but I'm not completely unarmed. I've been carrying a stiletto with me everywhere I go, a rusted specimen I discovered shoved into the back of a kitchen drawer at my apartment. I cleaned and oiled it, sharpening its blade until it could slice through a piece of paper like butter.

I know Dimitri's dead, but my paranoia didn't die with him. And if Pakhan changed his mind and sent one of his men after me, that man won't be going back to Russia.

He won't be going anywhere ever again.

Even more powerful than a human's instinct for danger is a mother's instinct to protect her child. Anyone who dares to threaten me will unleash the kraken of all mama bears. I'll carve him up like a Thanksgiving turkey.

I walk slowly away from the stall, ears pricked, eyes peeled, smiling like I'm a dimwitted tourist who fell off her Jet Ski, so dumb, clumsy, and injured that I don't pose a threat. At least that's what I assume whoever is watching me is thinking. Me with my broken arm and stitches. Me with my cute little paper bag of veggies.

Me with my knife hidden in the folds of my skirt.

Come and get me, if you dare.

I make a right turn onto a side street and leave the market behind. Picking up my pace, I head down the route I usually take back to my apartment, a shabby residential neighborhood separated from all the ritzy tourist hotels by railroad tracks and a high cement wall capped with barbed wire, its surface covered with graffiti.

At the end of the block is a small white adobe church, even more shabby than the houses. Slowly crumbling to ruin on a square parcel of dead grass, it has twin spires and a sagging roof. I know the side chapel door is left open all day and night, because I've been here to pray at every odd hour.

Hopefully the priest isn't inside. He thinks I'm a nice girl. I don't want him to see my claws.

I'll worry about how I'm supposed to get rid of a body later. I wish suddenly for Stefan and his skill in that area, and a bubble of hysterical laughter threatens to break from my chest.

I push through the creaking door of the church into humid gloom. It's stuffy inside, the air motionless and stale. On both sides of the simple wooden altar draped in white cloth, candles burn in metal tapers. Gazing down from his cross on the wall, a crucified Jesus sends me a look of heavenly disappointment.

"Don't judge me," I mutter. "I'm doing the best I can."

The church is composed of only a single large room with two rows of pews flanking the main aisle. There's nowhere to hide except in the confessional near the back, which, considering you have to be really close to someone to stab him, suits my purposes just fine.

Making a mental note to find a good therapist as soon as I get myself out of this mess, I hurry across to the confessional booth, open the door, and hunker down inside, closing the door quietly behind me. Then I wait, holding my breath.

For a long time, nothing happens. Sweat saturates the underarms of my dress. A fly drones lazily overhead, bumping into the ceiling. I hear cars passing by outside, the occasional bark from a dog.

Then—a floorboard creaks.

My pulse skyrockets. My hands start to shake. Easing the blade from the pocket of my skirt, I suffer a moment of cold terror when I realize my palm is slick with sweat. What if I drop the knife before I can use it?

But in the next moment, that worry is transfigured into disbelief as someone opens the door on the other side of the confessional and settles himself inside.

I can tell he's a man, though the carved privacy screen between us hides his features. He's big, broad, and seems totally at ease, crossing one leg over the other and folding his hands over his knee.

"Go ahead, *bhrèagha*," comes an Irish brogue I'd recognize anywhere, "confess all your sins. But only if they're juicy. I don't want to hear any nonsense about how you took the Lord's name in vain."

I burst out of my side of the confessional and throw open the other door.

And there he sits, as smug as ever, smiling at me like I'm silly for being surprised at finding him there.

I shout, "Killian!"

"Aye, lass. Who'd you think it was, Father Christmas?"

He's dressed exactly as he was the first time I saw him aboard the *Silver Shadow*. Faded jeans, black boots, a white T-shirt stretched across broad pecs. Tattoos snake up and down both muscular arms and peek over the collar of his shirt. Days' worth of stubble shadows his jaw. The only thing different this time is that he's wearing a smile instead of that frightening scowl.

"Well, don't just stand there staring at me with your mouth hanging open. Either stab me with that knife you're holding or give me a hug, but hurry up about it. I've got a plane to catch."

I drop the knife but am unable otherwise to move. I'm rooted to the spot as if I grew there.

It's Killian. Here. In Mexico.

I blurt, "How?"

Understanding I mean how is he here, how did he find me, he chuckles, shaking his head.

"Everyone keeps asking me that. I'm a *spy*, that's how. And obviously extremely intelligent, though of course I'm too humble to mention it."

Unfolding his long legs, he rises from the booth, then stands gazing warmly down at me. "You look a right mess."

"You should see the other guy."

He throws back his head and laughs, a bass rumble that echoes through the empty church, startling pigeons in the rafters into flight. "Aye, I heard about that. You'll be pleased to know you've earned quite the reputation in certain circles. In fact, I think it's safe to say that I'm not the only one who's legendary."

"Certain circles? You know people in the Bratva?"

Something shifts in his hazel eyes. A light goes subtly dark. It's a small thing, but distinctive, like the sun passing behind a cloud. He says, *"Ya vsekh znayu."*

I know everyone.

His Russian is perfect.

Through my shock, something makes me glance down at his hands. At those tattoos on the backs of his fingers. Skulls. Letters. Flowers.

Pakhan had the same tattoos.

My skin does the crawly tingling thing again, that animal sense of recognition. I whisper, "You know Pakhan."

"Oh, stop looking at me like that. You know I'm not here to kill you."

He sounds irritated, as if he's insulted I would think such a thing. I actually wasn't thinking anything of the sort. I was trying to piece together the puzzle of who he actually is, but now I'm reeling from another mindfuck because the English sentence he just spoke had absolutely no Irish accent whatsoever.

When I just stand there gaping at him, he smiles. Still without any accent, he says, "You have no idea how much I love being able to surprise you."

After a moment, my mouth remembers how to form words. "You . . . you're not Irish?"

"Nope. They're a wonderful people, though. Friendly, charming, great sense of humor. They randomly break into song a little too often for my liking, but nobody's perfect."

"But . . . but . . ." I blink an unnecessary amount of times.

He scratches his chin, looking at the ceiling and pretending to be thoughtful. "So the reason I wanted to see you is that I've been thinking about that kiss you promised me."

In spite of my shock—of all the shocks he's given me—I have to smile. *This* version of Killian I know. "I never promised you a kiss, you boob."

He tries to look offended. "You certainly *did*. Don't try getting out of it just because you were half-conscious and doped up at the time. A deal's a deal."

I start to laugh, weakly at first, then with more gusto as the insanity of my life hits me. I drop my face into my palm and laugh until Killian's arms close around me and he gently draws me against his chest.

He lowers his mouth to my ear and murmurs, "Are you all right? That's all I came to find out. And you better tell me the truth."

I answer into his chest, my cheek pressed against his sternum so I can hear his heart thudding beneath. "Or what, you'll punish me?"

He makes a disgruntled noise. "You said you forgave me for what I did on the *Silver Shadow*."

"I have, but that doesn't mean I can't give you shit about it."

He sighs. "Ugh, the language. Naz was a bad influence on you."

I fall still, then close my eyes against an explosion of pain.

Naz.

Oh God, that hurts.

Killian says softly, "Hey."

I look up at him. He's a little blurry because my eyes are welling with water.

"Everything's going to be okay. I promise."

I sniffle, shaking my head. "It's not. Don't you know what happened? He . . . Naz was shot, and he . . ."

I can't go on. I drop my head and close my eyes again, trying hard not to burst into tears.

His Irish accent back in place, Killian says drily, "Ach, *bhrèagha*. For such a fierce little thing, you're awfully weepy."

I jerk out of his arms and pound my fist on his chest. "Cut that out!" I shout. "Decide on one accent and stick to it! You're driving me crazy with that shit!"

He dissolves into laughter, clutching his stomach as he gives himself over to it.

"What's so funny?"

He drops the Irish act again, returning to speaking English with no hint of an accent. "You're two peas in a pod, that's all. That kid of yours is going to be a wild little Viking, running around screaming curses and breaking all the furniture in the house."

When I stare at him, pressing my hand over my belly, he stops laughing.

"Yes, I heard you're pregnant. And I'm truly happy for you." His eyes grow cagey, and his smile turns to a smirk. "But just because you've got a bun in the oven doesn't mean you can finagle your way out of that kiss you owe me."

"I can't kiss you right now. I'm deciding whether or not I'm going to pick up the knife and give you a few holes."

He kicks the stiletto with one of his big boots. It skitters away over the rough wood floor, far out of reach under a pew. Then he drawls, "I just decided for you. Now give me my kiss."

Exasperated with him, I stamp my foot on the ground and start to shout. "Killian! Tell me what the hell is going on! Tell me why you didn't return Stefan's phone calls and how Pakhan found out about the nuke and where you've been and what you've been doing since I last saw you and how you know I'm pregnant! And—most importantly—*tell me who the hell you are!*"

When he just stands there looking at me with his lips pulled between his teeth like he's trying not to laugh, I growl, "What?"

"You literally stamped your foot on the ground."

"So?"

"I've never seen anyone do that in real life. It's kind of adorable."

"Oh my God," I say loudly, glaring at him. "Naz was right. You really are the most irritating man on earth."

He waves a hand in the air. "Don't be silly. I'm amazing." Then he steps closer, so we're almost chest to chest. "Now. My kiss."

When I don't move, he taps his rough cheek. "C'mon. Just a little one here, then I'll tell you who I am."

I lift my brows. "You will?"

He nods, leaning closer. "Yes. Cross my heart." He turns his face to the side, waiting for me to kiss his cheek.

I huff out a breath. A peck on the cheek seems like a small price to pay for information, so I decide to do it.

But of course, Killian being Killian, things don't go as planned.

As soon as I rise on tiptoe and my lips are centimeters from his skin, he takes my face in his big rough hands and presses our mouths together. He kisses me softly, almost tenderly, cradling my face like a lover would. But he doesn't attempt to push his tongue past my lips, and he breaks away quickly. He smiles down at me as I shake my head and sigh.

"You lied."

"I'm a spy. It's a big part of the job description."

"So then you're not going to tell me who you are?"

He gazes at me for a moment, brushing his thumbs gently over my cheeks. Very softly, he says, "A friend, Evalina. I'm a friend."

He drops his hands and turns away.

"Hey!" I shout after him as he ambles down the center aisle of the church. "Where do you think you're going? I have questions! We need to talk!"

"Don't worry, you'll see me again sometime." He pushes one of the main doors open, then pauses with his hand flattened on the wood. Sunlight haloing his head, he looks back at me over his shoulder and smiles. "And I'll be keeping an eye on you, so you better stay out of trouble."

The door slams shut, but then opens up again not even a second later. Killian sticks his head back in. "Oh, and when you see him, don't tell him I found you first. That'll really drive him nuts."

He pauses for a beat, then breaks into a grin. "On second thought, definitely tell him."

"Who?" I say, confused, but he only winks at me.

The door swings closed, and he's gone.

TWENTY

EVA

When I run out into the street, Killian is nowhere to be seen. That son of a bitch pulled a Houdini on me, vanishing in a puff of smoke before I could force him to tell me who he meant by "him."

It dawns on me as I walk the rest of the way back to my apartment: *Connor.*

"Of course," I mutter to myself as I walk, lost in thought. "Tabby can find anyone anywhere. Somehow she discovered my assumed name. But how would that be possible? Only Stefan and the guy who made my ID know it, and neither one of them would talk. Maybe she saw my face on a security camera at the airport? Or maybe Killian's going to tip them off himself?"

Whatever happened, it's not safe for Tabby and Connor to speak to me. Not even with a phone call, no matter how brief. I'm not supposed to have any kind of contact with anyone from my former life, and if Pakhan somehow finds out that I did . . .

The phrase "heads will roll" won't be just a figure of speech.

I'm still wrapped up in my musings when I get back to my apartment. Distracted, I open the door and go inside, throwing open the windows to let the breeze in. It's a beautiful day, warm and sunny, the sky a brilliant azure blue, so I decide to go for a swim in the ocean to clear my head and think.

When I turn from the window, a dachshund puppy is sitting in the middle of my living room floor.

He's as brown as a walnut, with floppy ears, merry black eyes, adorably stumpy legs, and a little pink tongue that lolls out of the side of his smiling snout. From his collar hangs a silver name tag in the shape of a heart.

He yips, tail wagging, then starts to squirm and pant, wanting to play.

"Did you follow me inside, little guy?" I go over to him, my heart melting. I've always had a thing for wiener dogs, and this sweet baby is no exception. When I pick him up, he barks again, wriggling in my arms, and starts to enthusiastically lick my face.

"Okay, okay," I say, laughing and scratching his belly. "I love you, too, but let's see who you belong to so we can get you back to Mommy and Daddy."

He's squirming so much it's hard to get a grip on his little doggy tag, but after several tries, I manage it.

"Señor Sausage II," I say aloud, smiling. "Oh, that's so cute!"

My smile freezes when I realize I've met a dachshund with that name before.

It was in Cozumel, when Naz and I were taking a stroll down the street after seeing a movie. The night I first told him about Dimitri, when he promised to keep me safe. We saw a dog being walked down the street by his owner and stopped for a chat. When we asked the owner what the dog's name was, she replied, "Señor Sausage."

Then she told Naz he should get his wife a dog.

My heart starts to throb. My hands start to shake. A tremor runs through me, fine at the start, but quickly growing into a cascade of uncontrollable shivers.

"Don't tell him I found you first," Killian said, then disappeared with a wink when I asked who he meant.

My animal intuition is screaming at me now that he wasn't talking about Connor.

Cradling a wriggling Sir Sausage II against my chest, I uproot my feet from the floor and slowly, slowly walk into the bedroom, feeling as if my heart will pound right out of my chest.

It's empty.

The bathroom is, too.

There's no sign anywhere that anyone has been inside my apartment, but I don't believe in coincidences.

What I do believe in, however—what I believe in with all the pieces of my broken heart—are miracles.

And when I look out the window over the kitchen sink and see a beautiful dark-haired man standing out on the sand beyond my tiny fenced-in yard with his hands shoved deep into the pockets of a pair of ridiculous beige cargo shorts as he stares longingly at me, the powerful wave of emotion that rocks me is something akin to the euphoria of newfound religion.

TWENTY-ONE

NAZ

White-faced and wild-eyed, Eva stares back at me through the window. She's holding the dog so tightly against her chest I think she might snap him in two.

When he yips, she jumps, startled, but doesn't break eye contact with me. I can't break eye contact with her, either. Our gazes are fused together, burning and bare with emotion, so bare it's like standing naked with all my skin peeled off, every nerve exposed to the open air.

Then her face crumples and she starts to bawl. Shoulder-shaking, body-racking, gasping-for-breath sobs that have me breaking into a run to get to her.

When I throw open the door to her apartment and our eyes meet across the space between us, she's no longer able to stand upright. She sinks to her knees on the kitchen floor.

I fly across the living room to crouch and catch her in my arms, pressing my face to her hair as the puppy squirms between us, licking us both, barking with glee.

Eva lifts her head and stares up at me. Her face is red, wet, and the most beautiful thing I've ever seen.

"Beastie," she says in a ragged whisper, her voice strangled with emotion, her eyes bright with love and disbelief. Then she can't talk anymore and goes back to sobbing, her head dropped to my chest.

"I'm here, sweetheart," I murmur, stroking her back and trying to be careful with her because she's got stitches in her cheek and is wearing a cast on her arm—*a goddamn cast*—but my arms just want to squeeze her as hard as they can.

The dog squirms out from between us and starts to bounce and prance around us, pawing at our legs and barking like mad.

Then our mouths find each other. Our lips fit together like destiny, so perfectly right it was always fated to be. She kisses me back with a passion and desperation to match my own, clinging to me, her hand fisted in my shirt, making frenzied sounds deep in her throat as she arches against me.

When the kiss ends, we're both gasping. Crying. Shaken to our cores.

"You're alive," she whispers, reaching up to touch my wet face. "How are you alive?"

I say vehemently, "Because I'll never let anything come between us, sweetheart, not even death."

That sets her off into a fresh bout of sobs. "Th-the newspaper. Your obituary—"

"Fake. For Dimitri's sake, so he wouldn't think I was following. I didn't know you'd see it. I'm so sorry you saw it, that you thought—"

"He's dead!"

"I know—"

"And Killian—"

"He's the one who helped me—"

"The nuke—"

"We'll find it—"

"Pakhan already did!"

We pause our breathless, blurted confessionals to stare at each other, noses inches apart.

My heart beats so wildly it feels dangerous, like it might not be able to take much more before it bursts into a wet mess inside my rib cage. Anguish and longing and a fierce, superheated tenderness batter me from inside. Rage at her injuries claws at me. And beneath it all, the bitter taste of my own self-loathing and shame that I failed at the one thing I promised her over and over I would do: protect her.

Those stitches in her face and that cast on her arm are glaring reminders of just how expensive my failure was. God only knows what other horrors she endured, the kind of nightmares that leave scars. The *worst* kind of scars, ones that never heal and can't be seen.

Ones that fester, eating you from the inside out until you're as hollow and breakable as a seashell.

My arms shaking, I draw her against my chest. "I have so many things I need to say to you." I take a breath to steady myself. "There's so much to apologize for. So much to explain—"

Her fingers press against my lips, silencing me. She sniffles and dashes her fingers against her wet eyes. "No. No apologies. No regrets. We're both alive, and that's a precious gift. I refuse to squander it. I refuse to waste a single moment looking back on the wreckage behind us, because we have too much to look forward to."

She's looking at me with expectation, fervent love blazing in her eyes. For a moment, I'm so choked with emotion I can't speak.

Then she takes my hand and flattens it against her stomach, and this time the chest-deep, body-racking sobs aren't coming from her.

They're coming from me.

TWENTY-TWO

EVA

One month later

"Stop tickling me."

"I'm not tickling you."

"Seriously, Naz, you *know* how much I hate to be tickled."

He blinks innocently at me, fighting a smile. "I do know, which is why I would never!"

I try to glare at him, but it's impossible. I'm too happy to glare. His handsome face is inches from mine, resting on his pillow, and his eyes are full of love. We're lying in bed on a sunny weekday morning, our arms and legs entangled, our bodies still heavy with sleep.

Well, I *was* heavy with sleep until those treacherous fingertips wriggled into my ribs.

When they do it again, I jerk and shriek, making Sir Sausage II in his doggy crate at the foot of the bed start to bark with anxiety.

"I'm not kidding! I'll hurt you, mister! I'll take you down!"

Naz refuses to let me squirm away, instead caging me in the strong circle of his arms. Chuckling, he rolls on top of me, flattening me with his warm, delicious, masculine weight.

But I'm pretending to be mad, so I can't let him know how much I like it. "Oof. First tickling and now suffocation. Get off me, you ape. I can't breathe."

"Oh, you don't like me on top of you?"

I keep a perfectly straight face when I reply, because the glare I just attempted wouldn't stick. "Yuck. It's awful. I'd rather be doing anything else right now. Laundry. The dishes. Having a suspicious mole removed."

He kisses the tip of my nose and beams down at me. "Look at you, lying through your teeth. You're cute when you try to lie, you know that?"

I narrow my eyes at him, because I feel one of his hands creeping slowly around my waist. He's about to launch a surprise tickle attack, the bastard.

But I have my ways of distracting him, from tickle attacks or anything else.

Winding my arms around his neck and pressing my breasts against his bare chest, I kiss him deeply.

He does a full-body melt, like he always does when our lips meet. The entire muscular length of him softens, relaxes, his skin warming against mine. A small noise comes from the back of his throat, a sigh of pleasure and arousal, of deep, visceral need.

"No fair, Thelma," he says in a husky voice, breaking away for a moment to gaze down at me, his eyes hot and half-lidded.

My smile is saccharine sweet. "Excuse me, Dudley, but as I recall, *you're* the one who told me that all's fair in love and war."

"That's a ridiculous cliché," comes his prompt, mock-offended reply, "and Superior Man would never utter such nonsense."

I rub my toes against the tops of his feet, stretching my legs and luxuriating in the feel of his body aligned so snugly with mine. His big, hard, manly body.

Did I mention hard?

I whisper, "Hey."

He nuzzles his nose into the sensitive spot just below my earlobe and draws in a breath to steal my scent. "Yeah?"

"I think something has come between us."

His laugh is half snort, half chuckle. "You think?"

"Yes." He peppers a trail of featherlight kisses along my throat. "We should probably talk about how we're going to deal with the problem."

He raises his head and looks at me, dark brows lifted in twin quirks. *"Problem?"*

Loving the feel of his erection trapped against my belly, trying to look very serious and concerned, I rock my hips against his. "Yes, Dudley. It's a big problem, *quite* big, and if I may say, it seems rather . . . urgent. We should discuss the solution."

His smile is lazy, sexy, and sends shivers of delight all the way through me.

"You're right. We should discuss the solution to our . . . problem. Like adults."

He shifts his weight so his erection slides down between my thighs, then bends his head and takes one of my nipples into his mouth. He sucks until he gets the small gasp of pleasure he was waiting for. Then he moves his lips to my other nipple and lavishes that one with attention, too.

My voice comes out breathy. "Yes. Ahem. I think . . . oh." I pause for a moment to revel in the feel of his teeth lightly pressing down on the sensitive nub. "As I was saying, I think—since you're so awfully heavy—that I should get on top of you and ride the problem to its conclusion."

"I see. A very logical solution. Hmm. Let me think about that."

His tongue laps and laps at my taut nipple. His hand drifts down between my legs and begins—very lightly, palm flat—to rub.

When I make a muted sound of pleasure and spread my thighs wider, he slips his thumb between my folds and begins to slowly circle my clit with the roughened pad. It earns him a low moan, which makes him chuckle again.

He whispers hotly into my ear, "I have another solution to our problem, Thelma. Wanna hear it?"

His thumb swirls round and round, slippery now, going a little faster. I'm beginning to pant. He doesn't wait for an answer.

He decides to show me instead.

Sliding quickly down the length of my body until he's kneeling between my thighs, he bends down, tosses my legs over his shoulders, and puts his amazingly talented mouth—his hot, wet, talented mouth—right at the center of me.

I arch and moan. My eyes slide shut. Pleasure and happiness explode like fireworks throughout my body.

"I love that you love to do that," I whisper breathlessly, rocking against his mouth. "Oh God, I love it so much—"

My words are cut off by another moan, this one louder, when he slides a thick finger inside me. All the while his clever, clever tongue is dissolving me into a puddle.

My fingers clenched in his hair, I come, crying out his name and thrashing. Before my orgasm is over, he climbs up the length of my body, positions himself between my hips, and thrusts inside, cupping my ass in one hand and cradling my head in the other.

He kisses me deeply, passionately, letting me taste myself as he drives into me over and over again, our hearts pounding hard against each other's, the rhythm of our bodies perfectly matched.

When he falters, his arms shaking, husky little moans working from his throat, I know he's close but trying not to go over the edge. We lie still for a moment, just kissing. Long, unhurried kisses that are intimate and incredibly hot, especially since he's still buried inside me.

He hides his face in my neck. I slide my palms up his back, reveling in the feel of rippling muscles under my hands.

"I love you." His voice is hoarse, achingly raw, constricted with emotion. "Eva, I love you so goddamn much."

It brings tears to my eyes. "I know, Beastie," I whisper. "I love you, too."

And I do. Sometimes so much it hurts to breathe. I love this man, and will until the day I die.

"Sweetheart. Why are you crying?"

Naz's tender voice is an arrow piercing my heart. He kisses my wet cheeks, tightening his arms around me.

I have to take a few deep breaths before I can answer him. "I almost can't believe we got it."

"Got what?"

"Our happily ever after. Sometimes I feel like I should pinch myself to see if I'm dreaming."

"You're not dreaming, love," he murmurs, gazing down at me with tears in his own eyes. "And it's only gonna get better from here."

"Do you promise?"

He manages a crooked smile. "Superior Man gives you his word."

"Okay, then." I pause, smiling up at him. "But our problem still hasn't been solved."

He *tsks*. "Such a taskmaster! I can't believe I hitched my wagon to such an unbearable, bossy shrew!"

"Hitched your wagon? What are you, ninety years old?"

He presses his hips into mine, angling himself deeper, his eyes flaring with heat. He growls, "Does that feel like I'm ninety years old to you?"

My laugh is throaty with pleasure and joy. "No. Excuse me for the terrible insult to your ginormous ego, Superior Man. I sometimes forget how fragile it is."

He flexes, puffing up his chest. "Fragile? Ha! There isn't a single thing fragile about *me*, baby. I'm Teflon. I'm stainless steel!"

I try not to roll my eyes, because it will only set him off. Instead, I pull down his head and kiss him again, putting my heart and soul into it, giving him what he needs.

He gives it all back to me double.

❧

It's hours before we finally rise from bed, but we've got an important appointment to keep, and I don't want to be late for it.

The doctor's office is a pleasant twenty-minute walk from the apartment. When we arrive, I sign in under my assumed name, and we sit in the cramped waiting room, smiling goofily at each other in our hideous matching plaid chairs.

"So, Thelma," says Naz, crossing his tanned legs. He's sitting across from me, taking up all the space in the room with his presence, that powerful masculinity that had the pretty young receptionist wildly batting her eyes at him when we came in. Not even his stupid cargo shorts can diminish his appeal.

I keep threatening to burn them all, but he knows I won't. The dumb things are actually growing on me.

"Yes, Dudley?"

"What's your prediction? Boy or girl?"

My face flushes with pleasure. He's smiling at me broadly, the big handsome papa bear, so proud. "Boy, I think."

"Yeah? Why's that?"

"He's been making me sick for weeks. Probably wearing cargo shorts in the womb."

"Ha. You should work as a comedian."

"Oh, didn't I mention it? I got a job on a cruise ship doing just that."

There's an older woman with a magazine a few chairs down who glances up and frowns at me over the rim of her reading glasses. She's not happy with my choice of employment.

"Did you now?" Naz's tone turns stern, his smile fading. He knows we have an audience. "And when were you going to tell me about this?"

I shrug, as carefree as I can make it, feeling the woman's gaze on me sharpening. "I'm telling you now. I should probably also let you know I'm leaving tomorrow. We set sail for Europe at nine a.m. sharp."

"*Europe?*" Naz pretends outrage. "You're taking my child out of the country?"

I flip my hair and stifle a yawn. "Norway. I've always wanted to see the fjords. And I haven't even had this stupid baby yet, so calm down. I can go wherever I want without your permission."

From my peripheral vision, I see the woman's face turning red. She snaps her magazine, crossing and uncrossing her stout legs in growing agitation.

Naz and I fake glare at each other, both of us trying not to laugh.

He says, "No, you *can't* go wherever you want. I'm the father. I have rights."

I produce a dramatic teenage groan, flopping back in my chair and sighing. "You're not the boss of me, man. And I'm not going to let this baby get in the way of my *dreams*, you know? I mean, I'm seriously considering putting it up for adoption. Who needs this kind of commitment? Babies are a drag. Hey, is there a bar nearby? I could really use a martini."

The woman sucks in a sharp breath, rustling her magazine into a flurry. Luckily, the receptionist calls us in to see the doctor, because otherwise I think I'd have a tabloid slapped across my face.

Naz pinches my ass as the door to the waiting room closes behind us, leaning down to whisper, "Think she'll call social services on you?"

"Definitely. We should get in and out of here quick."

We're shown into the doctor's office, a space obviously made for little people with little feet. Naz is too large to fit comfortably. He keeps bumping into things until he finally just stands against the wall, flattening himself when the doctor comes in so he doesn't get smashed by the swinging door.

"Thelma. Nice to see you again."

The doctor is the same one who put me on prenatal vitamins and took off my cast. Her name is Flora, and she insists on being on a first-name basis with her patients, especially the ones she suspects have been victims of domestic violence.

When Naz came with me to have the cast removed, her icy stare almost froze off his face.

He smiles pleasantly at her now and is repaid with a slight narrowing of her eyes.

"Doctor."

"Sir."

No first names there. I feel bad for him, but I'm too excited to dwell on it. "Where should I go?"

Flora gestures to the cushy blue reclining chair covered in thin white paper next to a small desk. The desk holds a computer, a keyboard and monitor, and various other medical devices, the most important being the transducer that will capture the sonogram of my uterus and transmit it to the screen. It's a small plastic wand, not much larger than a computer mouse.

"Lie down there, please, and lift up your shirt. I'll be applying some jelly to your skin to help with the imaging. It might be a little cold."

I hop up on the chair and follow her instructions, lifting my shirt and pushing my skirt down to my hips so she has ample access to my belly. My still-flat belly, which the doctor tells me will start to swell in the second trimester.

I can't wait for that. I look like a crazy person now, walking around cradling my nonexistent bump like I've got a bad case of indigestion.

"Okay. Here we go."

Flora puts on a pair of thin blue gloves, then spurts a big blob of jelly from a tube onto my stomach.

She lied. It isn't "a little" cold, it's the temperature of an iceberg. I yelp, shivering.

"Sorry."

She doesn't sound sorry, but I forgive her because her smile is warm. Then she sticks the transducer wand into the pile of goo and smears it around, slathering it over my stomach in a big, sticky mess.

A murky black-and-white image appears on the computer screen. It looks like nothing. Like an alien landscape. A dark cave with some blobby white ghosts floating around.

I squint, trying to make out a shape. "What are we looking at?"

"A head."

Naz's voice is hushed and reverent. I glance over at him. He's still flattened against the wall, but now his eyes are like saucers. He's gone pale, and his hands are shaking.

I look back at the screen. "Where? Which blob is the head?"

The doctor points. I still see nothing. It all looks like bits of dim sum floating inside a bubble.

Then the doctor hits a key on her keyboard, and a strange sound fills the room. A weird underwater sound, fast and erratic, like someone randomly knocking on a door in a submarine.

"Is that my bowels?"

"That's the baby's heartbeat."

I almost fall off the chair. So loud it can probably be heard down the street, I shout, *"The baby's heartbeat?"*

When I look over at Naz, tears are streaming down his face. I hold out my hand to him, and he stumbles over, knocking aside a rolling metal tray and sending instruments flying.

He gasps, "The baby's heartbeat." We stare at each other with our eyes wide open, listening to the miraculous sound as if it's trumpets from heaven signaling the arrival of a host of angels.

"Oh," says the doctor.

The surprised tone of her voice almost gives me a coronary. I jerk upright, hollering, "Oh? What *oh*? What does that *mean*?"

She looks first at me, then at Naz. She takes her sweet goddamn time before saying, "There's more than one heartbeat, folks."

Crushing my hand, Naz collapses on top of me. He shouts, "The baby has *two hearts*?"

She's a professional—I have to give her that. In the face of two screaming lunatics, she remains patient and calm, looking back and forth between us with only the slightest weary exhalation of disgust. "No, sir. There are two fetuses. You're having twins."

All the air is sucked out of the room.

After an eternity, Naz whispers, "Twins."

I turn my head and meet his gaze. His stunned, loving, blissful gaze, in which I see my beautiful future.

⟨⟩

We walk back to the apartment in awed, shell-shocked silence. When we get there, a gorgeous floral bouquet is waiting for us on the front steps. Bright and colorful, it features sunflowers, Hawaiian ginger, and daisies.

Naz plucks the attached note from the bouquet and reads it, then starts—quietly—to laugh.

"What is it, honey? What does it say?"

Shaking his head and grinning, he hands it over to me without another word, opening the door and taking the bouquet inside. Sir Sausage II greets him with gleeful barking.

I look down at the note and read.

Dear Naz and Eva,

Congratulations on having twins. I can say from personal experience that twins are God's gift from heaven. I won't be at all surprised when you name the boy after me.

Killian

"The boy?" I shout to no one in particular. "One of the babies is a boy? How the hell does he know *that*?"

When I hear the sound of nearby laughter, I spin around, but find no one there.

Then the only one left laughing is me.

EPILOGUE

Naz

A year later

I'm not a religious man.

Don't get me wrong—I definitely believe there's something out there bigger than me. Bigger than everybody. Some infinite intelligence that directs the universe and started this whole gig a bazillion years ago. An energy we can tap into if we pay attention, if our hearts are open enough to let it in. But I'll never be the guy who goes to church to sing hymns and kneel in pews to pray. You won't catch me quoting the Bible or making the sign of the cross over my chest.

I don't need to do that stuff. Me and the force some people call God have an understanding now. It's simple and to the point, the way I like things.

I believe in him. He believes in me.

We're cool, me and that universal energy. And at times like these— watching Eva through the windows of her dance studio teaching ballet to a class of little kids—I feel that energy blaze through me so scorching hot and dazzling I might as well be Moses's goddamn burning bush.

She glances over and catches me watching. As it always does when she sees me, her face lights up in a smile.

It's beautiful, that smile. Considering everything we went through to get where we are today, that smile is nothing short of a miracle.

I lift a hand and grin back at her, then tilt my head to let her know I'll come in around back.

She blows me a kiss, then turns her attention back to the kids. To her left, parked against the mirrored wall, a double-wide gray stroller holds a pair of dozing babies, swaddled in yellow blankets.

Eva said yellow is a gender-neutral color. She didn't want to buy half pink stuff and half blue stuff, and she also said it's silly for people to have to dress their kids according to outdated ideas about masculinity and femininity anyway. What I got from that is that if my son someday decides he wants to wear dresses, and my daughter decides she likes army boots and pinstripe suits, we're gonna say "Sure" without batting an eye.

I mean, isn't that the whole point of love? That it's unconditional?

It is for us, at least. Because we both know only too well that once you start putting restrictions on love, you're not talking about love anymore.

True love doesn't come with any catches.

Eager to get my arms around Eva, I trot around the side of the brick building and down the short alley toward the back. It's a warm and sunny morning in Los Cabos, more humid than usual, the sky a perfect, cloudless blue overhead. As soon as I round the corner into the back parking lot, I stop dead in my tracks.

Then I start to laugh.

"Well, well, if it isn't the annoying spy."

Lounging against the wall next to the back door of the dance studio, with one booted foot kicked up against the wall, his tattooed arms folded over his chest, his head tilted back and his eyes closed, Killian smiles. "The *amazing* spy," he corrects, his Irish accent thick. He turns his head and looks at me. "How many times do I have to tell you that, mate?"

I chuckle and walk over to him. He pushes away from the wall and straightens, grinning at me, and we shake hands.

It's a crushfest. I'm certain my pinkie is broken, and I'm sure his is, too, but we just keep grinning at each other like the idiots we are, neither one of us willing to be the first to let go.

"Probably the same amount of times I've told you to stop with the fake accents," I say. "Aren't we past that at this point in our relationship?"

"Habit," he says, cracking a bone in my wrist.

In return, I squeeze harder and am gratified to see his left eyelid twitch. "Thanks for keeping an eye on them while I was gone."

Dropping the accent, he says, "Anytime. How'd it go?"

I'm starting to lose the feeling in my arm, but I'd rather be shot than release my grip first. "The kidnappers were sloppy. We found the girl in just a few days. It was an easy job."

Killian has a suspicious new twinkle in his eye. "'Course it was. Metrix is the best at finding people."

I stop shaking his hand—but don't let go of it—and glare at him. "If you're trying to tell me you had anything to do with us locating that kidnapped girl, I'll probably punch you in the throat."

He throws back his head and laughs. Then he releases my hand and gives me a friendly shove in the shoulder. "Oh, the temper! I'd forgotten how much I enjoy being threatened by you." He sighs dramatically, as if his feelings are hurt. "Even though I always volunteer to watch over your family when you have to leave the country for work."

Flexing my wrist, I grouse, "I said 'probably.' And we both know exactly why you volunteer, you ass, so don't pretend you're a saint."

He shrugs. "If you were really worried about it, you wouldn't keep asking me."

He doesn't even have the decency to look ashamed that I know he's still got a thing for my woman. But he's right: I'm not worried about it. Eva thinks of him as a big brother, and for all his egotistical and unscrupulous ways, I know he'd never cross the line.

The asshole is actually a gentleman. I wouldn't admit it, not even under pain of death, but I trust him.

Despite the fact that the man doesn't exist in any meaningful sense of the word.

According to Tabby, he's left no trace of himself anywhere. No fingerprints, no DNA, no verified name or date of birth. He's not even in the CIA or National Security Administration's database, which made Tabby think he possibly erased himself from the inside.

The only concrete thing she had to go on were the tattoos on his hands. Tattoos she discovered are shared by a dozen prominent men in international leadership positions ranging from organized crime syndicates to politics to business. There are no outward links between any of the men other than the marks on their knuckles, but all of them are powerful, connected, and what Tabby described as "morally ambiguous."

She said they're all bad guys who do good things. Or was it good guys who do bad things? Either way, apparently Killian is part of an unnamed underground network focused on keeping checks and balances on the *really* bad guys who do *really* bad things.

In other words, he's an antihero.

A term a little too cool for my liking, especially considering the bastard looks like every teenage girl's perfect bad-boy fantasy.

Ugh.

Seeing my expression, Killian laughs again. "God, that face. If looks could kill."

"You'd be dead a thousand times over," I say without heat. "Are you gonna come inside and say hi or what?"

He squints up into the sun. "Nah. You can tell Eva I said hello."

"She'll be pissed."

"She'll get over it."

"Suit yourself." I pause for a moment. "And thank you."

When he slants me a look, his lips in a wry twist, I say seriously, "I mean it. Thank you, Killian. You're a good friend."

He tilts his head and examines my face, his brows drawn thoughtfully together. "Friend," he repeats, as if he's unfamiliar with the word.

I roll my eyes. "Oh, for fuck's sake, brother. You can have a friend and still be a badass superspy dude."

His brows shoot up. "You think I'm a badass superspy dude? And you called me 'friend' and 'brother' in the space of two sentences? Are you about to confess you're in love with me? Because I think you're very nice, but I'm really not into that sort of thing—"

"Call me nice again and I'll knock your block off."

He smiles. It oozes satisfaction. "Better. I'm more comfortable with threats."

"You better get comfortable with having a friend, man, because you've got one whether you like it or not."

His smile fades. For a moment we merely gaze at each other, until he says, "Huh."

He seems astonished. Good. "Yeah. Deal with it. And you know this shit works both ways. You need me, you call me, I'm there. Got it?"

If I didn't know better, I'd think he was getting a little misty eyed. But then he turns his head and squints into the sun again and goes back to being his usual annoying self.

"I don't need anyone's help," he says, waving a hand dismissively.

Chuckling, I say, "Okay. Good talk. See you soon." I clap him on the shoulder in farewell and turn away.

I'm opening the door to the ballet studio when I hear him say, "It was the Germans."

I turn back and eyeball him. "The Germans? What're you talking about?"

He hooks his thumbs into the belt loops of his jeans and nods. "I'm talking about how Dimitri found Eva."

My blood runs cold. Metrix is still running ops with the Germans. Whenever he needs assets in Europe, Connor calls Günter and the gang. I shut the door slowly and stare at him.

"But . . . they're friendlies. Connor's worked with them for years. They're not the sharpest tools in the shed, but they've been vetted."

Killian shakes his head. "I told you a long time ago, Nasir, you never know whose side people are really on. Günter and his gang hire themselves out to the highest bidder. They have no country, no ethics, no allegiance to anything but cold, hard cash. It took me a while because they're extremely careful, but I've got ironclad evidence."

I think of the prissy little German who said they stopped to eat because he was hypoglycemic the night Dimitri took Eva from the apartment in Vienna. I think of him saying Günter knew people in high places, of how Günter himself was so calm and confident when he went out to meet the police . . .

They were playing both sides. *All* sides.

"Mother. *Fucker.*"

Killian grimaces. "Yes, probably that, too. I was going to take care of them, but I thought you might like to do the honors."

Thinking of everything their betrayal led to, my blood begins to boil. I curl my hands to fists. "You're goddamn right I do. Send me whatever evidence you've got, as soon as you can."

"Will do. Now if you'll excuse me, I have to get back to saving the world. Give *bhrèagha* my regards."

"That reminds me, asshole: I looked up that word. I know it means 'beauty.'"

He sends me a bland stare, which I return with a smug smile, my anger with the Germans momentarily pushed aside.

"In *Scottish* Gaelic, not Irish Gaelic. You need to research your foreign language pet names a little better."

Now he looks disturbed. "Really?"

"I wouldn't bullshit a bullshitter."

After a moment of gazing at me in silence, he says sourly, "How long have you been waiting to throw that in my face?"

My smug smile turns into a grin. It's so rare I score a point on him, I'm gonna savor every moment of it. "Don't sweat it, brother. I won't tell anyone you're not perfect."

He shakes his head, sighing. "And you say *I'm* annoying."

Then he turns and saunters off, throwing me a cocky salute over his shoulder. I watch him go until he disappears around the corner of the building, probably to vanish into thin air.

Or admire his reflection in a windowpane.

Still grinning, I go inside the back of the studio. Piano music floats to me from down the corridor, and I break into a trot. I've only been gone a few days, but even a single night apart from my family makes me twitchy.

Oh, who am I kidding? Even an hour away makes my chest ache.

When I hear Eva's voice, my heart starts to pound.

". . . and plié. Turn your foot out, Blanca. *Júntalos. Sí, bien.* Bend, now straighten . . . *ponte derecha.* Good!"

Her Spanish is getting better every day. She conducts the class three times a week in a mix of English and Spanish with the help of a friend she made at the driving school she enrolled in before the twins were born. Her students—mostly girls between the ages of four and eight—adore her, and she adores them right back. She loves kids. In fact, she's already said she wants more right away, even though the twins are only a few months old.

So of course I'm doing my damnedest to make that happen.

And I'm *extremely* dedicated to the task, if I do say so myself.

I pause for a moment inside the corridor that opens into the large sunlit studio, just to give myself the pleasure of admiring my woman. She's facing her students with her back to me, her attention on all the little girls in pink and white leotards lined up at the barre.

Barefoot, in a white chiffon shift that floats around her slim legs as she moves and her sun-kissed hair cascading over her shoulders, she looks like an angel.

She *is* an angel. *My* angel. Fierce and sweet, strong and brave, the beautiful soul with a heart so good the devil himself couldn't even make a dent in it.

And not for lack of trying.

"¡*Hola, Señor* Naz!"

One of the kids spots me and starts waving like mad. Then everybody joins in. A dozen little girls start to jump up and down and wave, screaming hello in unison.

Eva whirls around, her skirt billowing around her legs. She leaps toward me with bright eyes and a laugh and falls into my outstretched arms.

"You're back early!"

Closing my arms tight around her, I nuzzle my face into her neck and suck in the scent of her skin. The scent of home. My voice comes out husky, with a slight tremble. "I came straight from the airport."

Her laugh is low and throaty. She presses a kiss to my temple and whispers into my ear, "Missed me, did you?"

I pull away slightly and smile down into her beautiful face. "Now, *Thelma*, you *know* I can barely stand you, so let's not get carried away, okay? I came straight here because . . ." I flail around for a halfway plausible explanation. "I've decided I need to give this ballet thing a try."

"Oh?" Eva quirks her brows, her eyes dancing with laughter. "At your advanced age, *Dudley*? Won't that be hard on your joints?"

I give her a firm, close-mouthed kiss, muttering darkly, "I'll give you hard, woman."

She throws back her head and laughs. "Don't I know it."

The pianist, an elderly woman with narcolepsy who often falls into an abrupt sleep in the middle of class, clears her throat. When Eva and I look over at her, she's gazing at us over the rim of her glasses, her mouth pinched like a prune.

She's used to our public displays of affection, but that doesn't mean she approves of them.

"It's all right, Eva. I'll finish the class."

Inez, the friend Eva made at driving school, walks up to us, smiling. She's a compact brunette with a sweet face and a disposition to match.

Eva says, "Are you sure?"

"Yes." Inez sends me a conspirator's wink and lowers her voice, glancing toward the piano. "Go home before you give Señora Garcia a fit." She turns back to the class of little girls and launches into some instructions in Spanish, motioning for Señora Garcia to resume the music.

I don't wait for anybody to change their minds. I grab the stroller and Eva's hand and get the hell out of there, desperate to get my woman home and out of the wisp of a dress she's wearing.

Sir Sausage II is sunning himself on his favorite patch of rug near the living room windows when we come in. Hearing the front door open, he rolls onto his back, stretches, gives a sleepy bark and a tail wag as a greeting, then yawns and closes his eyes.

Eva calls to him, "Daddy's home! Come say hi!"

In response, we get another yawn.

"That animal is part sloth." I shut the door with my foot, balancing a baby in each arm. Eva's ahead of me with the stroller and the bulky diaper bag, a giant purse slung over her shoulder. She could be a Sherpa with the amount of stuff she hauls around.

"Are you hungry?" she calls over her shoulder, dropping the purse and diaper bag onto the long wood bench in the hallway. "I can make us some food."

As she's folding the stroller, I walk up behind her and give her a kiss on the back of her head. "Yes, Daddy's hungry," I say into her hair, my voice a growl. "And not for goddamn food."

She turns around, softly laughing, to scold me. "*Language*, honey."

"The twins can't understand what I'm saying yet." I beam down at the bundle in the crook of my right arm. Lucky for her, Sofia has her mother's rosebud mouth and wide-set eyes, the same petal-soft skin. "Can you, sweetheart?"

When the baby coos at me, waving her tiny fists, I turn to the bundle in the crook of my left arm. "What about you, Nico? Can you understand Daddy's potty mouth?"

He's fast asleep, so his only answer is a line of drool creeping down his chin.

With mock despair, Eva says, "I still can't believe I let you name our child after a rock star. Who I haven't even met!"

"Excuse me, but that rock star happens to be my best friend. And you know we're working on the logistics of a visit, so quit your yammerin'."

"Well, don't come complaining to me when your son hits puberty and starts putting together his gang of groupies."

This is a well-worn topic between us, one we both pretend is a sore subject, but we actually enjoy it. Because we're weird like that.

"Just because he's named after a famous musician doesn't mean he's gonna become one. And in case you've conveniently forgotten, our agreement was that *you* could pick one name, and *I'd* pick the other."

"Yes, and I named Sofia after my mother. It's a family name. You could've chosen a family name, too!"

I deadpan, "You're right. I should've named the baby after my father." I pause dramatically. "Zouhair."

We both look at the baby. Eva says tentatively, "I mean . . . he could grow into it?"

"Do you have any idea how long it takes to grow into a name like that?"

"Probably a hundred years."

"Exactly. Nico works right outta the gate. End of discussion. Now let's put these kids down for a nap, woman." I drop my voice. "Because Mommy and Daddy need a nap, too."

"A nap?" says Eva innocently, taking Sofia from me and cradling her against her chest. I follow her as she turns and makes her way, hips swaying, down the hallway to the twins' bedroom.

When our family expanded, we moved into a bungalow near where the old apartment was. I have a feeling that by this time next year, we'll be moving again.

If I get my way, we'll keep expanding until we need to move into a place the size of a hotel.

Eva continues in the same light, innocent tone. "You know, I slept really well last night. I'm not feeling tired at all. In fact, I was planning on doing a little gardening this afternoon. Maybe catch up on some paperwork, too."

Sassy little wench. I reach out and pinch her bottom. She yelps, laughing.

"Okay, boss man. Maybe a short nap is in order."

She throws a coy glance at me as she goes through the door.

I have to laugh, because we both know "short" means however long the twins will stay down, which could be hours.

Parenthood hasn't put a damper on how much we crave each other. We've just become pros at making the most of whatever alone time we get.

We make quick work of changing diapers and getting the babies settled into their cribs. Then we stand side by side and gaze down in awed silence at the gorgeous little faces we made. All those perfect little fingers and toes.

I know I'm the luckiest man who ever lived. There's only one thing missing from the puzzle, a single piece that will make my happiness complete . . . and though I had it all planned out, this moment feels too holy to let it pass.

I say quietly, "I've got something for you."

Eva's chuckle is dry. "I know you do, cowboy. Keep it in your pants for a second longer."

"I'm not talking about that."

She turns to me with a question in her eyes. When she sees how intently I'm looking at her, her expression turns alarmed.

"Oh God. Hurry up and tell me before I think the worst."

"Reach in my pocket."

Eva rolls her eyes. "Honey. Did I or did I not just tell you to keep it in your pants? We're in the babies' room, for goodness' sake!"

"Woman," I say firmly, turning her toward me and taking her face in my hands, "do as you're told for once and reach. Into. My. *Pocket.*"

Her look sours. But then a miracle occurs, and she relents.

"Fine. Since this particular pair of pants you're wearing only contains two pockets, and not the usual twenty-two, I'll reach. But if you've got a hole strategically cut somewhere, mister . . ."

My heavy sigh makes her smile.

But when she reaches into my right pocket, her smile freezes in place. She feels around for a moment, her eyes widening.

Gently cupping her face in my hands, I say, "I know you didn't want anything big, but I couldn't help myself."

Slowly, her hand shaking, she withdraws the little black velvet box from my pocket and stares at it.

She didn't want to walk down the aisle with a big belly, and a courthouse was out because she said her mother would roll over in her grave if she knew her only child hadn't been married in church, so we'd agreed we'd wait until after the twins were born to discuss it further.

Well, it's after. And I can't wait anymore.

I lightly touch my lips to hers and whisper, "Eva. My love. Our souls are already bound together. My life is bound to yours, and so is my heart, for eternity. Let's make it legally binding, too. Marry me."

Tears silently stream down her cheeks. She sniffles, then whispers, "I feel like I should look at this ring first before I give a definite answer. Because if your taste in jewelry is anything like your taste in clothing—"

I crush my mouth to hers and give her a kiss neither one of us will ever forget.

Mostly because she starts sobbing in the middle of it and shouts, "*Yes!*"

Which jolts the babies from sleep, so they start crying.

Then all of us are crying, but Eva and I are laughing through our tears.

ACKNOWLEDGMENTS

What a journey this was. I bled and rooted for Naz and Eva through three books, and now that it's done, I'm sad and happy, exhausted and exhilarated, and very much looking forward to them having all the joy and peace they deserve. God knows they earned it.

Thank you to my wonderful editor at Montlake Romance, Maria Gomez, for your tact, professionalism, and support. I appreciate you more than you can imagine. Melody Guy, my developmental editor, you are a genius and someone without whom my books would be nowhere near as good. I appreciate you, too, so much. To my team at Montlake and Amazon Publishing—including the copyeditors, proofreaders, marketing department, and everyone who works so hard there—a sincere thank-you for all you do to make my work better and get it into the hands of readers.

And speaking of readers, I wouldn't have a career without you, so thank you to everyone who purchases this book and to all my longtime readers who say such kind things about the people I make up in my head. I will continue sharing my stories for as long as you're interested in reading them.

Thank you to my parents, who were both voracious readers and instilled in me a lifelong love of books, and to my husband, Jay, who is the cornerstone of my life and the best man I've ever met. I never would have written twenty-one novels without your unwavering confidence in me. Your patience and good cheer are such blessings.

A final thanks to Sister Mary Claire, who taught my catechism classes long ago. I know you thought I was an irreverent lost cause, but your lessons about the grace of God helped shape the only deeply religious character I've written. Eva's faith gave her strength—probably the same kind of strength it took you to answer my endless heretical questions. Turns out, I actually listened.

ABOUT THE AUTHOR

 J.T. Geissinger is the bestselling author of *Dangerous Beauty*, *Dangerous Games*, and other emotionally charged romance and women's fiction. Ranging from funny, feisty rom-coms to intense, edgy suspense, her books have sold more than one million copies and been translated into several languages. She is the recipient of the Prism Award for Best First Book and the Golden Quill Award for Best Urban Fantasy and is a two-time finalist for the RITA© Award from the Romance Writers of America. She has also been a finalist in the Booksellers' Best, National Readers' Choice, and Daphne du Maurier Awards. She lives in Los Angeles with her husband and her deaf rescue kitty, Ginger. For more information, visit www.jtgeissinger.com.